James McComb is the author of *Truth and Lies* (2017), The *Spiritualist* and *Athens* (in preparation). He lives in Wales.

DREAMS AND DECEPTIONS

DREAMS AND DECEPTIONS

James McComb

Kestrel Books and Gallery
2021

Kestrel Books and Gallery
2 Garth Felin, Brook Street
Hay on Wye HR3 5BQ
www.hay-kestrel.com

copyright © James McComb 2021
All rights reserved

First published 2021

ISBN 978 1 874122 38 8

Printed and bound by Short Run Press, Exeter

Contents

The Poetry Girl	7
That Summer	11
Amongst the Girls	16
The Weatherman	34
The Artist	38
The Phone Call	42
Coloured Hair	48
The Man by the Lake	54
Night	72
Horses	76
Mary Mary Quite Contrary	79
Dear Charlotte	86
Xeno	91
Anatolia	95
The Devil and Amelia	100
Dr F	103
Athens	107
Malvern	111
A trip with lbc	117
Rosa	121
Manesh	125
The Gardens	129
The Runner	133
The Gallery	138
My Father's House	142
Epithalamion, Tunis, August 1971	146
The Rough-Legged Buzzard	150
Helene	155
Three Suicides	157
Badu Badula	160
Irene	164
Problems	167
The Neighbour's Wife	169
Budapest	175
The Island	180

For Rick and Annabel

The Poetry Girl

'Is it you?' she said. 'Are you in it?'
'Yes.'
'Who are you?'
I showed her my name on the contents page.
'Are they all poems?'
'Yes.'
'That's great.'
She smiled and held out her hand.
'Hi, I'm Chess.'
'Hi.'
'Do you want a smoke?'
'Okay.'
We walked up the Mound towards the castle. She walked sideways, kind of floating, her body turned towards me while she talked. She had long blonde hair and a pale, heart-shaped face. She was wearing a red and blue spangled waistcoat, white trousers and spangled slippers.
'It's just that I've got this grass and need someone to smoke it with.'
Below us, in the pleasure gardens, a guitarist was playing 'First Girl I Loved'. Above us an almost full moon floated in a blue-black sky. Tall, craggy buildings loomed over us. The castle, dark and brooding, was away to our right.
'Where are you from?'
'London.'
'I'm from Dunbar.'
'Dunbar?'
She smiled. 'It's nowhere really. It's not London anyway. It's just

Dreams and Deceptions

off the A1, heading east. Easy to miss. I'd like to go to London.'
We turned right at the top of the Mound and found a secluded spot beneath the castle, out of sight of the tourists. We sat down with our backs against the rusting gunmetal of an ancient cannon. From our eyrie among the lank, gloomy buildings we looked down at the twinkling lights of Princes Street and the New Town. She rolled a joint.
'Do you write poems?'
'No. Well, I have done, but they're no good. I think it's wonderful to be able to write.'
'It's nothing really. It's just writing down what you feel.'
'Yes but how do you know what you feel...in words, I mean? I mean, obviously we know how we feel. But – how do we know what words describe our feelings?'
She lit the joint and inhaled. The sweet smell of grass rolled up into the night air. She closed her eyes for a moment then let the smoke trickle out of the sides of her mouth.
'I mean, how do you know?' She handed me the joint.
'How do I know what?'
'What words describe how you feel. What the right words are.'
'Well...you just use the words you use. You just use the words that seem right.'
She sighed.
'Yes but what if the words never seem right?'
'Then it's not art.'
She smiled.
'Touché! Nothing like putting someone in their place.'
'Hey, I didn't mean that.'
'No, but you said it.'
I inhaled, felt the grass melt into my head. I closed my eyes, relaxed into the chemical change. There was no hurry. It was warm for the time of year, warm enough to sit out on a January evening. Below us the people in Princes Street were moving like ants, ever restless, never still. To our right the National Gallery glowed in its sea of light.

'They're like seeds in the wind. Everybody must get stoned. Isn't that what Dylan says?'
She laughed.
'Words again! There's no escaping them.'
She was leaning back against the cannon, her eyes closed. For a moment I thought she'd fallen asleep. Her mouth drooped as if with sadness, half-open, a dewdrop of saliva glistening on her lip. Yet she was younger than me.
I needed to get back to my pitch. My friends were waiting for me. I wanted to kiss her.
I said,
'What do you do?'
She opened her eyes.
'Me?'
'Yes.'
'I'm at art college.'
'So, you're an artist?'
'Not really. It's something to do, isn't it? I'm not an artist.'
'What sort of art do you like?'
'O – well, collages, that sort of thing. I don't have any special talent. I enjoy photography. I enjoy making constructs.' She made the shape of a square with her hands, then laughed again.
'I'm not very good at explaining myself. I'm sorry.'
'You don't have to explain yourself.'
'You know what I mean.'
I wanted to kiss her but I had to go. I was supposed to meet my friends back on Princes Street. I wanted to take her with me but I couldn't. I wanted to see her make shapes with her hands and her mouth.
She sat up suddenly and rubbed her hands together.
'It's cold.'
'Yes.'
I looked at my watch.
'I have to go.'
'Do you? Can't you stay?'

Dreams and Deceptions

'I have to go, really. My friends are waiting. They'll wonder where I am.'
'Can I give you my phone number?' She hesitated for a moment.
'Or aren't we into that yet?'
'Okay.'
She rummaged in her bag, found a crayon and a scrap of paper. Then she gave me a sly look.
'Or perhaps I shouldn't.'
'Why not?'
'How do I know what you'll do with it? Perhaps you'll sell it on the internet.'
'I won't sell it on the internet!'
'How do I know that? I don't know anything about you.'
She was looking at me half-smiling, half-sly. Her eyes were bright and her mouth inviting. Black clouds drifted across the face of the moon then drifted away again. I leaned across, brought my mouth gently down onto hers. She opened her mouth and closed her eyes. We shared saliva, exchanged fluids. I put my hand behind her head.
She opened her eyes. Watched me watching her.
'Stay a bit longer,' she said. 'I'll roll another joint. I feel comfortable with you. I feel like I know you.'
'I can't. My friends are waiting.'
I stood up. A black-backed gull, swooping low, nearly crashed into my head.
'Okay.'
She scribbled her name and number on the scrap of paper: *Chess, Dunbar 2215*.
'I bet you don't call me. But I will read your poems. Maybe you'll write about me one day.'
And she was gone – drifting down the Mound towards the bright lights of Princes Street, sideways, kind of floating, her long hair flowing in the wind.

That Summer

All through that summer Jamie and I played in the fields and hay-barns of his father's farm. An old retainer, Mr Cutler, disapproved of our antics and once reported us to Jamie's step-mum for messing up the hay in the barn. But she was cool.
'What exactly happened?' she asked Cutler.
'Well, ma'am, they messed up the hay good and proper.'
'In what way?'
'Well, the bales are all undone.'
'Can you not do them up?'
Officially we got a telling off. But she left us in no doubt that she understood what it was like to be a child, carefree and without responsibility.
'But don't do it again,' she said. 'We mustn't upset old Cutler.'
We ran back out into the fields, taking care to avoid Cutler's hay-barn.
You could say I loved Jamie as much as I loved myself. The thought of a world without him cast a shadow over me. I knew the summer would end and I would be sent back to school. I wondered what would become of Jamie without me.

All through the term I thought of Jamie. I wanted to send him a letter but didn't know how. I didn't know his address. Besides, he'd just think me a soppy girl, I knew that. So I repined alone.
One day the headmistress called me in.
'Your work this term has been poor. Is there anything troubling you?'
I knew she meant well. Some of the teachers didn't mean well

Dreams and Deceptions

but Miss Parker was okay. She had the interests of us girls at heart and, quite surprisingly for a teacher, didn't hate children. It was a chance to talk about it but still I couldn't bring myself to. It seemed almost crazy – I spent the summer running around the fields with a boy from a farm and now I'm all eaten up with love for him. I think, looking back, Miss Parker would have understood. But I didn't say a word.
'No, Miss Parker.'
She looked deep into my eyes but still I resisted her.
'There is something, isn't there? Did something happen in the holidays?'
'No.'
She knew I was lying. But she didn't push it. She just said, 'Well, if you change your mind and want to talk about it, come and see me. Anytime day or night. Whatever it is. It is not only your education that is my responsibility while you are here but your well-being – your development as a person. You can trust me.'
'Yes, Miss Parker.'

But things went from bad to worse. This aching for Jamie just ate me up. I thought – I could write, send a letter care of my own parents. But so could he. And he hasn't. Why not?
Then I thought, I'm just a stupid girl, what do I know?
Life at school had become a trial to me now. Nothing interested me – not my friends, nor my work, nor any of the other activities the school went in for. There was every opportunity for a girl like me. I wanted to get into photography – at least I thought I did – and the school had a state-of-the-art photo lab but when the opportunity came I didn't take it. I'd always been interested in art and was good at it – I was top of my art class – but now I couldn't be bothered. It just seemed pointless – green fields and blue skies and birds singing.
The world wasn't like that.
Instead I drew a sketch of a tired, haggard man with all hope lost and a dead look in his eyes.

'What is this?' said Mr Cadwalladr, the art master.
I shrugged.
'Just a drawing.'
'This isn't like you. Last term you were the best in the class. Now you produce this?'
I shrugged again. I didn't care what he thought. I didn't care whether or not it was any good.

Miss Parker called me in again. She got straight to the point.
'There's something troubling you,' she said. 'It's something you won't talk about. But your work is suffering. Everyone around you is suffering. As your headmistress, *in loco parentis*, I can't just stand by and do nothing. Please, tell me what's troubling you.'
'I want to go home,' I said, and at once the clouds lifted.
'Why? Don't you like the school?'
I started to cry and once I'd started I couldn't stop. I couldn't speak either. I just stood there with tears flooding down my face. I didn't just want to go home. I wanted to die.
Miss Parker came round her desk and put her arm round me. She led me to a chair and sat me down.
'Don't try to speak,' she said. 'You're okay. You will be okay. I'm going to help whether you like it or not. Okay?'
I looked her straight in the eye.
'No-one can help me. You don't understand.'
'Why can no-one help you?'
'Because the problem I have is mine, no-one else's.'
'A problem shared is a problem halved.'
'That isn't true.'
'It can be.'
'No, it can't.'
There was a silence between us.
'You're an unusual girl,' she said eventually. 'But I have a very high regard for you. I think whatever you want out of life you will get.'

Dreams and Deceptions

'You don't know what I want.'
'No. But whatever it is, I believe you will get it.'
'Maybe there's nothing I want.'
'Maybe. And if that's true, that's what you'll get.'

I went back up to my dormitory. I lay on the bed. I felt cold and almost immobile. So cold, so immobile, I thought I might die. I'd had what I wanted, my summer with Jamie. Now I wanted nothing. I didn't want to upset the school, or Miss Parker. I knew she meant well. But she didn't understand. Why should she? Who could?

By the end of term, I'd almost forgotten Jamie. I realised I'd built him up in my mind, built him up into something he probably wasn't. Laid all my trips on him, and he just a kid. He was the same age as me – twelve – but boys are way behind girls, emotionally, at that age. Why had I ever thought he might write – he probably didn't even know my name. To him I was just a stupid girl. He probably wouldn't even remember me.

I got off the train and there was my father in the stupid car he'd bought because he liked what it looked like in a magazine. I felt frigid. He stooped to kiss me. I didn't kiss him back.
We drove.
'Jamie's home,' he said. 'I saw him the other day. He was asking after you.'
I stared out of the window.
'Don't you want to see him?'
'Not particularly.'
'Oh?'
'How's work?'
'Oh, not so good,' he said, to my surprise. Usually my father never discussed such matters. Usually all that stuff was far too important for me.
'How come?'

'I've been made redundant.'
'You'll have to sell the car then.'
'It's not that bad. Not yet.'

Jamie came round once or twice that holiday and asked if I wanted to play but I told him no. I didn't give a reason – just watched the shadow of pain in his eyes. You put me through it, I thought – now it's your turn.
'Why don't you play with Jamie any more?' my mother asked me.
I shrugged.
'Dunno.'
'Don't you like him any more?'
'He's alright.'
I was dreading my school report, given all that had happened, but Miss Parker had said she'd look after me and she was as good as her word. Apparently, I'd had a difficult term, puberty and all that, but I was headed in the right direction. I was going to make it.
And that summer was dead and gone.

Amongst the Girls

Rosemary is sitting next to Steve. Her cheeks are crimson and there's a sly, slightly intoxicated smirk on her face.
She is wearing a short skirt and her knees are almost touching Steve's. Yet Steve pays no attention to her.
We are watching Peter Sarstedt on the television. He is singing 'Where Do You Go To My Lovely, When You're Alone In Your Bed?'
It is a favourite of ours. We like the song but we also like him. He possesses a very grown-up, very international moustache. He sings of the 'back streets of Naples' yet he also sings of Juan-les-Pins and St Moritz. He sings of the Rolling Stones, of Sacha Distel and the Aga Khan. He sings of 'carefully designed topless swimsuits', though why it is necessary to 'carefully design' a topless swimsuit – rather than just, say, take off the top bit – we do not know.
He conjures up a world we all wish to inhabit, a glamorous world of jetsetters and folksingers, of the rich and talented. When he sings about the topless swimsuit we all fall about laughing.
I laugh, Maxine laughs, Jade and Annette laugh. Rosemary does not laugh. She maintains her fixed smirk.
Her exposed knees. Her big thick woolly. She looks like a sheep.
Her outfit is all wrong. Too much on top, too little below.
Rosemary, we agree, needs a 'carefully designed' seduction outfit. To seduce Steve. Because Steve, it has to be said, is not the easiest girl in the world to seduce.

Vivian is magnificent. He is Suleiman the Great, Mussolini and

Pericles all rolled into one. He is six foot three, approximately, and as grave as a dictator; his moustache is almost as grown-up and international as Mr Sarstedt's. Where he got his moustache from I do not know. Perhaps he got it from his mum. His mum is Italian, big tall and blonde, whereas his father is a dark-skinned Arab. That's where he gets his good looks from. He looks like Clark Gable in Gone With The Wind. That is how we imagine him: gone with the wind. It is what we fear.

All we girls are in love with Vivian except for Rosemary, who's in love with Steve, and me.

Vivian has a younger brother called Squidge. His real name is Alex, but we all think of him as Squidge. He is the exact opposite of his brother: five foot eight to Vivian's six foot three and no moustache at all. He tried to grow a moustache but nothing happened. Or rather almost nothing. It would have been fine had nothing had happened. He would have remained as he was, bare-lipped. Instead bum fluff grew. Bum fluff! A disgusting term (we girls, generally, don't have bum fluff) but the only one that adequately describes it, that 'suits the action to the word' as Professor Sir William Allsopp, the old sea dog who is also my history tutor, would say.

But that doesn't stop Squidge chasing us girls.

When we fall about laughing as Mr Sarstedt comes up with his comical line about the swimsuit, which he does on a weekly basis (he seems to have been number one for ever), Squidge creeps over and starts surreptitiously feeling us up.

Our breasts and thighs.

In broad daylight.

Without asking.

It's outrageous!

If a girl's breasts and thighs aren't sacred, what is?

But if Vivian's there, who's going to complain?

We girls (with the exception of Rosemary and me) dream endlessly of Vivian. Feeling us up. Taking us out. And more.

Dreams and Deceptions

And so, when Squidge starts feeling us up, we just imagine it's Vivian.
Except that it never is.
It's not Vivian. It's Squidge.
Vivian-the-magnificent never shows the slightest interest in our breasts and thighs.
What's up with Vivian?

Rosemary's all dolled up, though you wouldn't notice. Rosemary's idea of dolling herself up is to cover her mouth with purple lipstick and wear the shortest denim skirt she possesses over tights.
Tights! I ask you.
Will Steve go for a girl in tights?
I don't think so.
Steve has a boyish figure and a nice rosy face with just the hint of a moustache. He, or rather she (for Steve, aka Stephanie, is actually a girl like us) likes to dress in men's clothes and adopt a deep, manly voice. Because of this, she doesn't speak much. She is always fighting the squeak. The girlish squeak that can pop out, like a little mouse, at any time.
How are you Steve?
Deep breath.
Affect deep drawl:
I-i-i-m f-i-i-ne.
But if you catch her unawares she talks perfectly naturally, though she's not a girly girl.
Less girly than me, anyway.
Steve doesn't notice anything funny about Mr Sarstedt's line about the swimsuit.
It passes him/her by.
Maybe he/she's seen too much of the world.
Maybe she/he finds the whole idea of women in topless swimsuits disgusting.

My own favourite is Aga, the Turk.

Aga is Harweg's best friend and, aside obviously from Vivian-the-magnificent, Harweg is the dominant male round here.

But Harweg is not like Vivian. Vivian is tall, elegant and handsome, a dead ringer for Clark Gable. Harweg is six foot tall but bulky. So bulky, in fact, that when he sits in one of the wooden chairs in the TV lounge it is prone to collapse under his weight.

It doesn't end there.

Not for him, clambering sheepishly, or smiling abashedly, from the wreckage. Heaving up his great bulk from the floor.

No way. He attacks the chair.

The chair splinters beneath him. Up he leaps – despite his bulk he is remarkably light on his feet – and turns in a trice in a full-blooded karate pose – one leg behind the other, hands raised, palms up, side on. Like a sidewinder ready to strike. He emits muffled verbal explosions – 'Pa! Pow!' – while he heaves to, one hand replacing the other, position-wise, in a blur, hands and feet acting in tandem, and smashes what's left of the chair to smithereens.

He is a homicidal lunatic.

Even Aga, who is also a homicidal lunatic, regards him with awe.

Aga is fierce with everyone but meek and mild with Harweg.

Besides which, Aga's the one for me. I like Vivian (who doesn't) but I prefer Aga. He is almost as tall as Vivian, and quite good-looking too, though, unlike Vivian, he has a silly side to him. For example, he will pretend to shake your hand but instead grab your thumb and twist it backwards until you cry out with pain. This makes him (as well as his victim) double up.

He hides things too, especially things belonging to us girls. Once he hid my bag for a whole afternoon. Another time he hid my pen. Once, worst of all, he hid my contraception.

Colin has a gritty, weather-beaten face (comes from all those hours rowing on the Thames) and lusts after Maxine. Maxine is the prettiest girl here (present company excepted of course).

Maxine is so tiny she has to eat platefuls of Complan every day just to maintain a presence on this earth. She has a sweet, pretty face. Also, surprisingly for such a tiny person, she is fearless. Colin is no match for her at all. What she sees in him I don't know, though it's not hard to guess what he sees in her.

Rastl is the worst of all of us. Rastl is a thief. Rastl stole my ring and my bracelet; and, when I took it off for a couple of seconds to sink my head into a basin of water, seeking a little relief from the pressures of the day, my watch too. It wasn't just any old watch either – it was my grandmother's watch. She left it to me in her will.

She wrote in her will:

'And to James I bequeath my watch. It was given to me by my grandmother, and now I bequeath it to my favourite grandchild, James. I impose no conditions upon this gift. James may keep it or sell it as she wishes. This is a decision for no-one but her.'

Of course various other members of my family tried to have my gran's watch off me – my mother, for starters, to pay for her next shot of morphine; my twin sisters, Catty and Caithness, who made the ludicrous claim that my grandmother had assured them the watch would be theirs (they worked on the principle of safety-in-numbers, that pair, before Yours Truly was even hatched).

How can two people share a watch? I wanted to say. It's absurd. But of course even saying it would have allowed for the possibility. So I kept stumm, except to say,

What's written is written. Right?

Take the watch and fuck off, said the twins. You'll get nothing else.

I don't want anything else, I said.

And now here I am. With Rosemary and Steve and Vivian and Squidge and Harweg and Aga and Colin and all the girls.

And Rastl.

Harweg is full of hot air. He claims, variously, to be a karate

Amongst the Girls

expert (viz. the chair business, though I say anyone can beat up a chair), the world's greatest lover (that's a laugh) and the fifth Beatle. Not officially of course: officially they are still the fab four, John, Paul, George and Ringo, not John, Paul, George, Ringo and Harweg. But only because 'Harweg' doesn't have quite the same ring to it. The same goes for the song-writing credits – Lennon-McCartney somehow sounds better than 'Lennon-McCartney-Harweg'. But it was Harweg who wrote or co-wrote them, he tells us, all the same. How come 'Lennon-McCartney' keep coming up with ace songs as if they were two-a-penny, eh? Well, it's obvious. It's Harweg. It's Harweg who wrote or co-wrote most of their famous hits – Paperback Writer, Strawberry Fields Forever, Hey Jude etc.

And what about all those tracks where strange instruments are played...who was playing them, eh? Do you think John, Paul, George and Ringo came up with all that stuff themselves? Seriously?

And that's not all. Pete Townsend wrote 'Tommy' all on his own? Don't make me laugh. Syd Barrett wrote 'See Emily Play'? Syd and Harweg are peas in a pod. Syd may be the front man, yes, and may have made a contribution. But the real work, the business-end stuff, is all Harweg.

Or so he says.

I asked him once, when we girls were laughing ourselves sick over the topless swimsuit stuff, whether Mr Sarstedt had really written his famous song or whether that too was the work of Harweg. Harweg didn't answer as such. But he smiled and winked and tapped the side of his neck.

He often taps the side of his neck.

Karate point, he says.

Harweg possesses a nylon-strung Spanish guitar and from time to time we encourage him to play. Usually it is, for some reason, inconvenient. A bad time. Or perhaps we are an unworthy audience. But once in a blue moon he does pick up his guitar and

Dreams and Deceptions

thrash out a chord or two. The opening to Tommy, perhaps, or some other Who classic.
He doesn't sing as such – just pushes out his big rubbery lips and make walrus noises. ('I Am the Walrus' – Lennon-Harweg – was all about him, he'd have you believe.) It's enough to convince most of us. Aga for example. And if Aga believes it, that's good enough for me.

Harweg is big mates too with Mick and Keith – he and Keith, apparently, are the real driving force in the Stones, Mick is just the front man. 'Street Fighting Man,' like 'I Am the Walrus,' is all about Harweg. For when Harweg is not at Abbey Road studios, putting the finishing touches to Sergeant Pepper or cranking out a few tunes for the Floyd, he is up West taking out hustlers and scalpers, three or four at a time, just for fun.
Who's going to shed a tear for hustlers and scalpers?
After a hard day's work at the studios, he points out, one needs a little fresh air and exercise.
When his chair broke, he was just reacting the way any fighting man would. After all, there could have been a gang of highly trained fighting men sneaking up on him from behind.

Aga himself is no slouch when it comes to fighting. He's six foot plus and has the bearing of the naval man his father, himself an admiral, has determined he will be. But in the presence of Harweg he turns into a quivering wreck. He follows Harweg blindly. All Harweg has to do is push out his big rubbery lips and make walrus-noises and Aga, like the rest of us, barring Vivian, just falls into line.

Monique has no time to sit about giggling at Mr Sarstedt. She is older and more grown-up than the rest of us girls and her uncle is the President of Peru. She has studied at the Sorbonne. While we're watching Mr Sarstedt singing about the jet-set life,

she's living it. She flies to Paris or Switzerland for the weekend and returns leaving a trail of broken hearts in her wake. In the evenings, she goes uptown, to clubs or discos, and hangs out with writers and artists and film directors.
One night she, Harweg and Aga decide to go uptown.
We're going uptown, says Aga. You can come. But you mustn't speak or do anything. Okay?
Why not? I ask him. But Aga's in no mood to compromise.
Do you want to come or not? he says.

We all squash into Aga's mini.
Aga knows how to treat a lady. His father, the admiral, has instilled in him not just a love of the sea but good manners. 'Manners are everything,' he told me once, just before bending my thumb back in his comical way and bringing tears to my eyes. At first, when I couldn't find my ring and my bracelet, I assumed Aga had hidden them. For days I badgered him, refusing to believe his denials. In the end he turned round and said,
If you ever mention your ring and bracelet again, I'll squash you flat. I haven't got them, you silly bitch. Right?
Like I said, Aga knows how to treat a lady.
Now he opens the door, not for me but for Monique. Like a seriously upmarket chauffeur. He would look good in a uniform with a peaked cap. He is opening the door, smirking, almost bowing, as this uptown bitch, with her cool cigarette, steps in.
Thank you, Aga, she says, in her heavy Peruvian accent, without even looking at him.

We are going to some gig in some club that Harweg has heard about.
Incognito, of course, lest Harweg's presence upstages the band (whoever they may be – not the Beatles or the Floyd, presumably).
Aga shuts the door with a flourish. Harweg hefts himself in on the passenger side (no room for a walrus in the back, Monique or

Dreams and Deceptions

no Monique). Aga gets into the driver's seat and I'm left standing on the pavement.

I clear my throat, in a manly way, but no-one notices.

I set off round the car in pursuit of Aga.

I am here, you know, I say.

His face is black as thunder but he reluctantly clambers out to allow me ingress.

So here I am, stuffed in the back of the mini with Monique (who doesn't address me once, just blows smoke in my face) while Aga decides to take on an E-type that's thrown down the gauntlet, or so he thinks.

Away we go, uptown, haring through the traffic, overtaking on the wrong side of the road and bouncing off kerbs.

Aga, I notice, doesn't once consult his rear-view mirror (personally I can't take my eyes off it).

He is not concerned with what was, only with what will be.

He's on the tail of the E-type as we approach the Hyde Park underpass and then, whoosh, he's round it in his souped-up mini and gone.

Now the E-type's on our tail.

I'm nervous as hell at all this carry-on. Monique's too cool to notice. Harweg's egging the idiot on.

Kick the shit out of the slimy bastard! he yells. Then he winds down the window and sticks his great walrus frame half out of the car.

We're going to have you, you slimy bastard! he roars.

He is the walrus alright.

We race through the underpass, zig zag zig zag, undertaking, overtaking, veering left and right to prevent the E-type (which has quite a bit more soup even than Aga's mini) from getting past us.

Harweg is gesticulating at the guy, making karate-like gestures with his hand and his forearm.

We're up and out of the underpass, bouncing over the bumps – actually flying through the air. But there's a queue of traffic ahead which neither Aga nor Harweg has noticed.

Amongst the Girls

You slimy cocksucker! Harweg is saying, whilst making his gestures.

The E-type guy actually looks pretty okay to me – young with rosy cheeks and curly brown hair. I wonder if he's a Peter Sarstedt fan. I wonder if maybe…

Crash!

Bang!

The bonnet's up and the car in front of us has been pile-driven into the one in front of it.

The E-type's skidded round us and is away, up Piccadilly.

Aga, with the engine smoking, reverses and shoots round the pile-up onto the wrong side of the road and sets off in pursuit.

The E-type's way ahead weaving in and out of the traffic. Aga has his foot down but, with the bonnet up, is driving blind. We hit the kerb, bounce back off, collide with a taxi, describe a complete circle and stop.

Smoke hissing and billowing from the open bonnet.

The taxi driver, a man of below average height and above average age, stands in the road. He is grinning.

Put the bonnet down, says Harweg.

Aga gets out and pushes down the bonnet. It bounces back up.

Bloody E-type.

Pure luck.

We were ahead.

I know.

What now?

Monique speaks, coolly flicking her cigarette out of the window.

This will do, she says, in her thick Peruvian accent.

She gets out and that's the last we see of her.

We drive on until the radiator's drained. We come to a halt in an alley in Soho.

Dreams and Deceptions

Aga and Harweg inspect the damage. The radiator grill is bashed in and steaming. The bonnet no longer shuts properly. One of the headlights is broken.

Aga kicks a tyre and curses.

My father will kill me, he says.

I slip my hand into his. It just seems the right thing to do. To show support. I know I'm not allowed to speak or anything, but I do not think a little reassurance, a little human comfort, will go amiss.

And besides, it's my big night out.

A little guy in a cap comes up. He has a weather-beaten face – actually, it looks like his face has been scrubbed raw by the wind – and carries a bottle in his hand. His speech is slurred.

Looksh like you shaps been in a acshident.

Fuck off, says Harweg.

No needsh to be like that.

Harweg turns to him, his great big turnip-face red with rage. His small eyes flashing. His small ears twitching.

FUCK OFF!

Okay okaysh. Okaysh, says the little guy, backing away, waving his bottle.

You shaps got no fucking reshpec! he says. No fucking reshpec!

I'll give you fucking reshpec! says Harweg. But Aga takes his hand from mine and gently pats Harweg's lapel. Almost like a lover.

It's not worth it, he says. He's just a drunk. Ignore him.

And this, amazingly, calms him.

Silently they sit day after day, side by side, like two lilies in a pond. If Steve gets up, to go to the loo, say, or powder her nose, nothing happens. Not a word is spoken nor a glance exchanged. Rosemary continues to sit as she sits, to watch as she watches. Maxine might bustle in and out, looking for her handbag, on her way to a date, or one-legged Michelle limp in, or even Annette with her net (sample dialogue: 'Do you sleep with a net?' 'Only when she lets me!'). But no-one occupies Steve's chair. No-one, that is, except the occasional male of the species. Aga did once but quickly retired, smiling, when he got the message. Colin did once too and then assumed everyone was picking on him (No we aren't Colin, honest; it's just that you and Rosemary aren't an item, right?). Rosemary herself stays stumm. Steve comes back from wherever she's been, plonks herself down in her chair beside Rosemary and crosses her long trouser-clad legs. Not a word is spoken, not a glance exchanged.

They are like two lilies, drawn together by magnetic attraction yet somehow never quite able to meet. Their attraction draws them this close but no further. Something makes them stop. Right there.

So near and yet so far.

Steve isn't a girl's girl. When she comes out with us girls she's always pulling a vanishing act. Sometimes within a few minutes of setting out, sometimes in mid-outing. But she always pulls it. We might be sitting in a restaurant, Au Pere de Nico, say, just us girls on a girls' night out, laughing and falling about and having a good time, and Steve will get up and leave.

Just like that.

I once asked Steve what her plans for the future were.

I want to be a train driver, she said.

The phone rings in the hallway. I happen to be passing. I pick it up.

Harweg?
Hello?
Is Harweg there?
No, I don't think so. Can I take a message?
This girl starts sobbing down the line.
I'm Diane, she says. Then she says, Can I trust you?
I put on my deepest voice. I pretend to be Steve.
Yes, I say. Yes, you can.
Can I really? Are you his friend, really his friend?

Dreams and Deceptions

Yes, I say, deep and manly.
I'm at the end of my tether, she says. He won't call me. He won't even give me his number. I had to get this number from directory enquires. I don't know which way to turn. I need someone to believe in; someone who'll believe in me.
Believe in me, I said. I'm your girl – er, boy.
I'm sorry, she says, still crying. I'm sorry. But I'm expecting his baby.

We fixed a date. We met over two helpings of raspberry cheesecake in the Air Terminal in Cromwell Road.
Diane was not what I expected. I'd expected some sad, dumpy little thing. I hadn't expected a raving beauty.
When I told him he just kicked me in the stomach. Over and over again. Karate kicks. To save money, he said. He tried to kill the baby.
I held her hand.
That's terrible.
But I still love 'im. It's crazy, I know. I don't know why. Whatever he does, I just can't help it. Did you know he writes all the Beatles' songs and is a member of the Who?
I knew he was in Pink Floyd.
Pink Floyd! wailed Diane.
I handed her a tissue. She dabbed her eyes.
She squeezed my hand.
Meeting you has really helped, James, she said. I'm so glad we've met. I've no-one else to turn to.
How about your parents?
They threw me out when they found out I was pregnant.
She wept and dabbed her eyes with a tissue.
Men are such bastards.
Yes, they are. Most of them.
I thought of Aga. What a prat he looked, standing beside his blown-up mini. And what a git he'd look in his naval uniform.
And yet we still love 'em, don't we? We can't help it.

Not necessarily. Not always. Not if they try to kill you or your baby.

It's his baby too.

Is it?

It has to be. I haven't slept with anyone else. She started crying again.

I squeezed her hand.

I just want…someone…to…you know…

Yes. I know.

I held Diane's long beautiful hand in mine. We looked into each other's eyes. Then I kissed her, right there in the Departure Lounge.

A voice said, very loudly,

Could passengers boarding the nineteen-fifty British Airways flight to Paris make their way to Departure Gate two.

Sounds like us, Diane, I said. Me and you. We could just take off.

Yes, said Diane, laughing through her tears. O dear. I hate laughing. It seems wrong somehow.

You have to laugh, Diane.

Yes, she said, looking into my eyes.

I kissed her again. Tongue to tongue.

Her lips were softer, her tongue sweeter, than I'd dared hope.

You're great, Diane. You know that? Miles too good for him.

She was melting.

I know.

We could run away together. Just split. Find somewhere to live. Have the baby, look after it ourselves.

Could we?

Yes. How are you fixed at the moment, living-wise?

I've got nowhere to live. She started crying again. He said he'd get us a place. Together I mean. The bastard. She sniffed and dabbed her eyes. Then, when I told him I was pregnant, he just kicked me in the stomach and left. I'm sleeping on a friend's sofa.

Dreams and Deceptions

Okay, Diane, I said, trailing the fingers of one hand through her lustrous blonde hair whilst holding her hand tight with the other. Give me a couple of days. I've got one last thing to sort out. Okay?

It was Monique who told me. Monique, the stuck-up bitch. Harweg's friend, Monique. Girl to girl.
Rastl's got your watch, she told me. And your bracelet. Now you know – but you didn't hear it from me. Okay?
Okay, Monique.
We girls have to stick together, right?
Right.
Rastl: number one creep. Slimebag of the first order. Eldest son of the chief of police in Teheran (he says).
He wasn't going to get away with it.
I asked Aga to help but he didn't want to know. He'd heard about me and Diane. He called me a 'dyke'. How's your car? I asked him.

So instead I roped in the old sea dog.
There was more to the old sea dog than met the eye.
He was the ancient Mariner reincarnate. With his skinny hand and fevered brow. His long grey beard.
He taught history, if 'taught' is the word.
He taught you, if you were a girl, one on one. In an attic up in the rafters. He and I, all through that long hot summer, until the Stones played in the park and everybody split.
He took your hand, if you were a girl. He gazed into your eyes. He stroked your knee.
He was sixty going on eighty.
He looked like the ancient Mariner.
By thy long beard and glittering eye
Now wherefore stopp'st thou me?
And I just a girl of seventeen.
We studied side by side while the sun poured down like honey

through the attic window and his hand rested on my knee. Like a comatose toad.
Music drifted up through the window from the street.
So I closed up my books, took his hand off my knee and looked into his glittering eye.
I need your help, Bill.
What is it, child?
Rastl, I said.

Rastl lodged with the sea dog. It was the way things were. We girls lived in one house, the boys in another.
That evening at six o'clock, when I turned up at Rastl's house and rang the bell, the old sea dog answered.
Where is he?
Second floor, first room on the right.
Turn a blind eye, I told him. You should be able to manage that.

No point knocking. I opened the door and walked straight in.
I closed the door behind me.
Hello Rastl, I said.
Rastl grinned.
You come see me?
I come see you, Rastl. I want my watch. And my bracelet. And, while we're about it, my ring.
Rastl shrugged and fastened his lying brown eyes onto mine.
What watch? What bracelet? What ring?
The ones you stole from me.
Me? I stole these things?
Yes, Rastl, you did. And I want them back. And you know what? If I don't get them back I'm going to report you to my uncle.
Your uncle? Who is your uncle?
My uncle is the chief of police.
He never! grinned Rastl.
Straight up, I told him. Just like your dad. With powers like his, too. You think I'm joking?

Dreams and Deceptions

Rastl continued grinning. He walked up to me and put his hand on my budding breast. He thought he could charm a lady. He was wrong. I kneed him in the groin, not once, but twice. Then, summoning up every ounce of my girlish might, I gave him a two-fister, straight in the chops.

Pow!

Rastl sat down on his bed.

So, what's it to be – my watch or my uncle?

Rastl's lip was bleeding. He took out a large, embroidered Persian handkerchief, dabbed his lip and inspected the blood. It was red and there was quite a lot of it.

Rastl was a thief. A small thief. Not a big thief, like Harweg or Aga.

He didn't have much choice.

Okay, he said. I give you your watch. He went to a drawer and opened it. His trophy drawer. As he did so, he turned slyly to glance at me.

Don't even think about it, Rastl.

Okay. You tell no-one. Okay?

He brought out my watch, my bracelet and my ring. For good measure, he brought out a state-of-the-art camera too.

Take this, he said. You not tell your uncle, the chief of police.

Keep the camera, Rastl, I said. Or, better still, return it to whoever you stole it from. By the way, you're a slimebag. Did you know that?

I had what I needed – my watch, my bracelet, my ring. Those things meant something once, when they were given to me. My mother drunkenly embracing me as she handed me the ring, desperate for her next shot; curly-haired Jamie slipping the bracelet on my wrist, age ten. And kissing me.

That memory will stay with me for ever.

One day I'll need it, I reckoned. When times get rough, as they surely will.

Amongst the Girls

I went to the Air Terminal with two tickets to Paris in my pocket and sat down to wait. She wasn't long coming – walking through the terminal towards me, a little fatter than before, but still beautiful. Beautiful and cool, like me.

The Weatherman

There is a depression coming in from the North Sea. I've seen the barometer. Last night there was an eighth of an inch of rain. The first measurable rain all week. But there will be more rain by the end of the week. You can tell from the swing.
He had lank, silvery hair and his subject was the weather. He had once got bored, he told me, of the usual inane exchanges on his subject, decided there was a gap in the market and turned himself into an expert. Everyone was interested in the weather, girls especially. People were surprised and impressed that he was able to discuss the subject in such intricate, mind-blowing detail. It was like, he hazarded, being a guru. They sat at his feet.
Girls?
They all do. But girls, yes.
We were walking on the mountain and I could smell rain though he insisted it wasn't.
No rain till the end of the week. Low pressure. He smiled. I've seen the barometers.
Aside from the hint of rain it was a beautiful day, a little cloudy but warm and clear. We could see the tops of the mountains. On some of the peaks there was still snow though it was August.
I told him about my travels and the different cuisines I had encountered. Cuisines were a particular interest of mine. There are three great cuisines, I told him. French, Turkish and Chinese. French we all know about, sauces, chips and so on. Chinese is different, everything chopped up and stir fried. Turkish is the least known. It consists mainly of beans and rice and little bits of meat floating in thick, mysterious sauces. Indian, I went on, is not a cuisine in itself, as it is simply meat and rice spiced to

The Weatherman

disguise the flavour. He let me talk, as happy to encounter my area of expertise as he was for me to encounter his.

I was reading *The Way of all Flesh*, sitting up late at night with a torch.

We could go down to the pub tonight, he suggested. With those new girls.

Two English nurses had arrived and he, in his friendly way, had instantly latched on to them. They had been impressed, in turn, with his command of nimbuses and precipitations, of lows and highs. It suited me fine. I would let him do the talking, just wait and see what happened. We drove to the pub, which was at the end of the valley, in the old Triumph.

Have you ever had Carlsberg Special?

The nurses giggled. We have.

No, I said.

It's a knockout, he said. He ordered a round. It had a thick slightly chemical taste. It was my round. My ears started behaving oddly, picking up snippets of conversation from all round the room, yet unable to focus on what was being said to me directly. He was keen for another. I went along.

The nurses sat that one out.

These things are potent! they said.

One of the nurses was slim and quiet, my type I reckoned. His was plumper and jollier, more like a sister. The quiet one put her hand on my arm.

Are you sure?

About what?

About having another. We have to drive back.

You can drive if you like.

She smiled and relaxed. Okay. I'm not sure though.

She was moving about in front of me and my ears had now latched on to a strange buzzing noise. I wasn't sure where this noise was coming from. I eventually realized it was the noise of human chatter, the noise of the pub itself.

I'm alright, I said.
I was seeing double. We got up and lurched out of the pub, stumbled towards the car and climbed in. The slim nurse, Annie, sat up in the front with me.
Do you want me to drive?
I can drive. I laughed gaily. You steer.
I manoeuvred the vehicle gingerly out of the car park and into the road. I drove slowly along the valley towards the hostel. Everything had a vapoury double: the mountains, the trees, the vehicles heading towards us. Annie had one hand on the wheel as the car meandered haphazardly along. Whenever headlights appeared from the other direction we steered towards the bank. When they'd gone we made for the safety of the middle. We started two rabbits that lolloped along in the headlights for a while then scuttled into the bank.
We reached the hostel.
Well, that was fun, said Annie. Thanks. See you tomorrow.
Right. See you tomorrow. Goodnight.

I went up on the mountain alone. It was another beautiful day, hotter than yesterday. The heather was crisp and warm. The mountains were still and beautiful, capped with snow. It was the highest point for miles around; the bluff of the high mountain loomed precariously above us, above the sea and the town.
I followed a trail inland, away from the hostel, right round the valley.
On the other side of the valley I saw a small bird sitting beside the path. It was a fledgling, unable to fly. It must have fallen from a nest, except there was no tree nearby for it to have fallen from. Perhaps it had been carried in the beak of a larger bird and fallen, or been carried by the wind. It wouldn't last long, sitting there on the ground. The first stoat or pine marten, fox or cat would have it.
I picked it up and held it in my hand. It was dying. It sat uncaring in my hand, too weak even to attempt flight. It looked

The Weatherman

straight ahead, bright-eyed, its throat quavering. It had no fear. Now, touched by human hand, it was condemned.

I thought of taking it home then thought better of it. I made a nest for it in the grass and left it. I walked round the mountain under the blazing sun, relieved to be alone, except I couldn't get the bird out of my mind.

Life is short and sweet, I thought. Death is part of it.

I could still feel the bird in my hand, like the ghost of an amputated limb.

The Artist

She came into my shop and started looking at the books on the shelves. Under her arm she had a pad of A3 drawing paper. She was a student or an artist.
 Are you an artist?
 I'm trying to be.
 It was nearly time to close the shop.
 Where are you going?
 Home. Do you want to come?
 She was blonde and blue-eyed, intense and beautiful. We walked across the park in darkness. I told her about Margarita, the woman I loved but from whom I was separated, and something about myself. She told me something about herself too although, she claimed, there was less to tell: 'You're so much further on than me.' We held hands as we crossed the park, then climbed over the fence and went through the back alleys to the house.
 We sat in the kitchen with Judy and Rob. I made tea and rolled a joint. We listened to music and talked. We ended up alone in my bedroom, the turntable still clicking round.
 Will you sleep with me?
 Sleep with you?
 Yes.
 Why?
 I hate to sleep alone.
 Okay.
 She took off all her clothes off except for her pants and I took off mine. She had big, soft, pendulous breasts. We got into the bed. I leaned over and kissed her on the mouth.

Goodnight, Jennifer.
Goodnight, James.

She was sleeping beside me. I leaned over her and whispered,
I want to make love to you.
Her eyes opened. She was looking up into my face.
What?
I want to make love to you.
I thought you just wanted to sleep with me?
No, I want to make love to you.
 She sat up, suddenly wide awake, her big breasts swinging free. Stared at me gravely with her big blue eyes. Then she put her arms round her legs and lowered her head to her knees. She stayed like that for a while then turned to look at me.
I'm sorry, she said. You must think me so stupid.
No.
I'm sorry.
No. I'm sorry.
I put my arm around her.
I'd better go.
 I climbed off the bed and stood between her and the door. She brushed back her hair with her hand, looking at me.
Please don't go.
No, I must.
 She went next door, still naked apart from her pants, to the small balcony room that had once been Jill's.

We were sitting in the park. She was wearing a long green velvet dress. Her gold cross sparkled in the late summer sunshine, flat between her half-exposed breasts.
 What do you want out of life – or should I say, what do you think you want? Nobody really knows what they want. They think they want this when they want that or that when they want this. In the end they get nothing, neither what they want nor even what they don't want. Just nothing, an absence. Religions

Dreams and Deceptions

talk of 'the middle way' as though that were some sort of ideal. Really, it is just the environment that permits us to survive. Survival is everything. Survival through reproduction. Survival through sex. But why should we wish to survive – especially when we know we won't? What is it that binds us here so strongly, that causes us to do anything to survive? Is it fear? Is it love?

I flipped a brace of cigarettes out of the packet, lit them, handed one to her.

I want to be an artist. I don't want babies.

Why?

I don't know. I just enjoy painting, that's all.

Anyone can enjoy painting. A child can enjoy painting.

A child can be an artist. Whatever anyone does is art, whether it's good or bad. That's what I believe.

No, it has to be good. It can't be bad. If it's bad it's not art, it's just...nothing. Self-pity. Special pleading.

I don't think so.

I thought her the most beautiful woman I'd ever seen. Her blonde hair framing her gentle, intense face. Her blue eyes touched with innocence. The gold cross that glinted between her breasts. The sunlight framed her, picking out the strands in her hair, lighting up her smile.

You're beautiful.

Why do you say that?

Because it's true.

How can it be true? You know it's not true.

She was looking at me as though beauty were an objective fact, not simply an expression of love. I wanted to tell her I loved her. To take her in my arms and hold her. I wanted to say, All my life I have been looking for someone like you.

I said, Because, to me, you are.

Our love had no chance. Left to ourselves it might have. But Margarita came back like a force of nature, barging past her in

The Artist

the corridor, knocking her sideways then standing in the middle of the kitchen like a conquering empress.

She was alone in the back room, the room that led to the garden, the room with the piano, sitting on the bed. I sat down at the piano and played 'Sad-Eyed Lady of the Lowlands':

With your mercury mouth   *in the missionary times*
and your eyes like smoke   *and your prayers like rhymes*
and your silver cross   *and your voice like chimes...*

Your saintlike face, your ghostlike soul...
I understand.
No, you don't.
She turned her blue, childlike eyes to mine.
I'm in love with someone else, I said.

The Phone Call

The phone rings and rings.
    He hangs up.
    He takes a deep breath and calls her again.
    The phone rings and rings. Someone picks up.
    Hello?
    Hello?
    Sam, it's James.
    O.
    Didn't you hear the phone?
    No. It doesn't ring. There's something wrong with it.

Phones do not actually ring. The ringing you hear when you call a number, and before somebody answers or the line goes dead, is not actual ringing but simulated ringing. A mirage, like simulated water. Though you may lie upon the desert sand you cannot drink.

    So why did you pick up?
    O, she says vaguely. I was going to call someone.
    Me?
    No, not you.
    Are you still there?
    Am I still here?

Is she still there. Yes, she must be for she is at the other end of the phone. Where else could she be? But that is not what he meant. What he meant was, are you still there, living there, and not living with Taylor.

The Phone Call

How's Taylor? he says.
He's fine, she says. As far as I know.'
As far as you know?
I haven't seen him all week.
Well no, she wouldn't have. He is living there, she is living here, at the end of the phone.
Would you like to meet up for a drink? he says.

It is, to him, an important question. Would she like to meet up for a drink. If she wouldn't then nothing would happen. If she would, anything could happen. Probably would. Things being as they are, with Taylor.
With Taylor?
With Taylor?
Yes – you mean, with Taylor?
No. I mean, if you like. But what I meant was – maybe we could meet for a drink. Just you and me.
Why? she says.

Another good question. So many good questions. His, hers. His are better really, more immediate and to the point. Hers are as a dreamer's, meandering.
Why not?
I'm quite busy this week.
Are you?
Yes.
Doing what?
O, you know.
He doesn't know. He doesn't have a clue. What could she be so busy doing, there on the other side of London, staying with her sister? How could she possibly be busy in her sister's house on a summer's day on the other side of London?
What's wrong with your phone? he says.
I don't know. It just doesn't ring. We can ring out.

43

Dreams and Deceptions

That must be frustrating.
Not really.
How about Thursday?
Thursday, she says dreamily.
Yes. Maybe that pub in Sloane Square, what's it called.
Sloane Square, she says.
Yes, the pub in Sloane Square. Opposite the Royal Court. Right on the corner. The Fox and something.
On Thursday?
If you're not too busy.
I'll have to see.
Why?
Well, I'm not sure.
About Thursday or about meeting?
About Thursday.
Well, you better decide. I can't call you again. You won't hear the phone.
Okay, she says. Thursday.

She is, has always been, vague and dreamy. He parks his motorbike, attaches his helmet to the lock and walks towards the pub. Sloane Square is full of people – flower vendors, late night shoppers, office workers travelling late, pleasure-seekers travelling early. London hurtling like a comet through space towards its uncertain destination. The travellers keep moving as travellers must. Will she even be there? He thinks she will. Whatever else she is, she isn't a liar. If she says she'll be there, she'll be there.

He stands for a minute outside the pub. Then he sees her.
You came.
So did you.
Well, I was always going to come.
True.
They drink for two hours. The conversation flows quite

The Phone Call

easily — he can't pounce on her in the pub. She talks about her parents, the American novelist father she never sees, the mother she rarely sees though she lives in the same city. Her sister. Taylor.
    Poor Taylor. He doesn't really know what he wants.
    And you?
    Me?
    Do you know what you want?
    I want to find some man to look after me, she says.

Outside the pub he pushes her up against a wall and kisses her.
    Well, she says. That was a surprise.
    Yes.
    I wasn't expecting that.
    Nor was I.
    It was quite nice though.
    He does it again. This time she pushes him away.
    Too soon.
    Too soon?
    Yes, too soon.
    When then?
    O, I don't know.
    It's now or never.
    Is it?

He has known her for three years, ever since his girlfriend introduced them. Sam and Taylor. But Taylor was a sot and prone to losing his temper. He would never lose his temper. Now Taylor was away. He took her to movies and pubs and every night they went back and slept in Taylor's bed. She was as vague and dreamy in bed as out but still he couldn't get enough of her — feasted on her long languid body that at times seemed made of marble. Then she went away on a pre-planned holiday with Taylor and discovered she was pregnant.

Dreams and Deceptions

She called him.
I can't see you again.
Why not? Is it Taylor?
Not really. Partly.
What then?
She couldn't say. They were like every other pair of travellers moving through the starry night not knowing where they were going.
We have to make decisions.
No we don't.
We do.
We don't.
She was working for a firm of architects just north of Holborn. He drove up on his motorbike, parked in a motorcycle bay, walked towards her office. They walked in the early autumn sunshine, the air still dry, the sun on their necks and arms. Autumn scents filling the streets and squares.
It's beautiful.
Yes, she said. I love the autumn colours.
What about us?
What about us?
You know I want you.
We have no future, she said. Though she was often indecisive, sometimes her mind could not be changed.
Okay, he said at last.
Okay?
Yes. We just go back to where we were. You and Taylor, me and Alice.
How is Alice?
She's fine.
And the baby?
He's fine.
I thought there was something wrong with him?
There is. But he's fine. Everyone has something wrong with them.

Do they?
Of course. No-one's perfect.
No.
He tried to kiss her but she turned her mouth away.

Coloured Hair

Mmm, you say. Delicious.

You open your mouth wide and introduce a chip. You eat it, lasciviously.

Mmm, you say. Lovely.

Time, I say, forking a piece of withered cabbage. Well, we are what we are, not what we were or will be. We are a succession of present-based selves. Strangers really. We may think we are linked to past and future selves but we aren't. Time is just a way of seeing things.

Mmm, you say, your eyes widening. Delicious.

Let's go home. I want to take you home right now and have you. In through the door, gear off, there and then. On the floor, up against the wall, no time to reach the bed…

Mmm, these chips really are good. Really good. Mmm. You dangle a chip from your mouth and slowly suck it in like you're sucking in air.

We don't die. The present comes to an end. But the ripples go on rippling outward until…

Like goldfish in a pond…

…the heron comes and eats them.

Jeez, it's terrible. I push my plate away. Why did we come here?

You wanted to come here.

I did not.

You did. You studied the place in your usual way and declared it 'fit for the purpose of lunch'.

I never did. You brought me here.

Coloured Hair

I never did.

You are smiling at me, your long hair tumbling down across your shoulders to your bony feet. Your long red hair. I remember wrapping myself in your hair and sleeping there for what seemed like days at a time.

Time, that old French duck.

It was other selves, other versions of us, back then, wasn't it?

What do you mean, 'back then'? When was 'back then', anyway?

When was back then, or what distance is it from...

Since we...

I don't know. Two years? Twenty?

Jeez, twenty years. Is it as long as that?

Besides, you didn't want me. You didn't want me then, anyway.

O, I wanted you. I just couldn't have you. So I thought, if I can't have you I'll stop wanting you. Do you remember Damien?

Of course I remember Damien. I was married to him for twelve years.

The waitress comes over.

Is it okay?

Is what okay?

Your meals?

No. The vegetables are overcooked and withered. Strung out, like dry beans. Where on earth did they come from?

Where did what come from?

The vegetables.

From Dorset.

O yeah, Dorset. Well they're withered and overcooked...and cold.

And yours? she says to you. How's yours?

Mmm, you say sucking in another chip. Delicious.

The waitress turns to me and delivers a radiant smile.

Dreams and Deceptions

You're cute, I tell her. How old are you?
Twenty-two.
That's a nice age. I was twenty-two when I met this woman here. Isn't she gorgeous? She was twenty-seven. She's always been five years older than me. Haven't you, sweetheart? Except when you were only four years older briefly in the eighties...
You smile at the waitress.
Don't mind him. He has funny theories about time. He thinks it goes in all directions at once. He's a bit of a philosopher.
I'm studying philosophy.
O, I say, who are your favourites?
Nietzsche. And Descartes. I think therefore I am. Yet who am I?
Heidegger?
With his whirlpools and eddies? His 'dasein'? It's all a bit heavy for me. I prefer the...
...pre-Socratics? But hey, you're cute. Really you are. Would you be willing to give me your phone number?
The waitress smiles.
No, I don't give out my personal number to customers. But you can always contact me here, at the restaurant. I work here every day, apart from Wednesday.

Old Father Time. What a fellow! With his grey beard and his scythe.
O I know. Yes, I do understand. She fancied you.
No, she didn't.
Yes she did. I could tell. She was coy.
She wasn't.
She was.
Alright, I'll put it to the test. When she comes back I'll ask her out. Then we'll see.
Go ahead. You'll find out I'm right.
Either way, she's too young for me.
Not for me.

Coloured Hair

My red-haired lover smiles.
Anyway, you like them young. You used to, anyway.
No I didn't. You were five years older than me.
But still young. Then.
We could have made it if...

Go home. Open the door. Breathe in the sense of anticipation. Of expectation. Devour it, like the scent of a rose.

Then, once we're inside, rip your clothes off fast, I'll give you a hand if you like, and get stuck in. Immediately. Perhaps we will stagger, perhaps I will carry you, naked, *à deux*, to the bedroom. Stagger, fall, collapse upon the bed. Or maybe we'll just do it on the floor, there and then. Or up against the wall. Or on the kitchen table. Flat on the kitchen table. Yes, that's it. Flat on the kitchen table...

The waitress comes over.
Have you finished?
No.
O, I'm sorry.
Don't be sorry.
Okay.
This woman – my wife – thinks you fancy me.
Does she?
She thinks I should invite you out. Would you like to go out with me?
Okay.
Okay?
Yes. When?
Tomorrow?

The waitress wrinkles her pretty nose and looks up at the ceiling.

No.
No?
No. Time has flowed back on itself. There is no tomorrow – not one distinguishable from yesterday anyway.

Dreams and Deceptions

You know, I've been here before. I remember it now. It must have been, what…around the time you and I got together. Back then. I came here with someone…

Karine?

No, not her. It was one of the ones you didn't know about. She was called Rosie, I think. Yes, that's it, little black-haired Rosie. We went for a walk in the park – I can't remember which one. She knelt down by the side of the lake and began to sing to the swans. She had a beautiful voice. The swans came from all sides of the lake to listen. Then she kissed me.

Lucky you.

It's not luck. What happens isn't luck. It's prearranged.

Who does the arranging – God?

Our chromosomes. Everything is written. We just act it out.

Like you and Rosie. What happened between you, anyway?

O, nothing. You know. The usual. We went back to her place and lay in bed naked caressing each other. I leaned across her and began to lick her…her mouth, her neck, her nipples…she didn't like it, I could tell. And that put me right off. We'd already had a few jars and, well, what with one thing and another…

I push my plate away.

Disgusting. Really horrible. What brought us here?

You did.

I did not.

You did. You studied the place in your usual way and declared it 'fit for the purpose of lunch'.

I never. You brought me here.

I never did.

You are smiling at me, your long hair tumbling down across your shoulders to your feet. I lean across the table, feel for your hand, kiss your cheek.

What's that in aid of?

Us. Time. The combination of the two.

It's too late for combinations.
It isn't. It's never too late for anything. Says the heron with his grey beard and the scythe over his shoulder.

The Man by the Lake

His memories existed in their own right, were not part of him, like emanations of the spirit or avatars of the soul. A boy who seemed to exist in his own right standing before him. The boy is smiling and his mouth is opening and closing though he makes no sound. A girl also stands before him, she stands beside her brother. She is moving, the boy is still. She is clearing away plates, she does not look at him. The boy continues opening and closing his mouth as the girl moves outside his vision.

Are these memories? How can they be? The boy and the girl are standing before him clear as day. They are not memories. They exist in the present not in the past. They are standing there, no

The girl is gone. Now she is back, moving past the boy, attending to something upon the table where

A woman is sitting. She is feeding a dog. The dog stands with its paws planted in the ground its mouth opening and closing yap yap yap   yet no sound emerges.

It is, he concludes, a silent movie. But why silent? Nothing else is silent.

His brain for example is not silent. It whirrs and thrums and snaps like a pencil and throbs like an engine. It squeals like a water rail. It breathes like the breath of a giant. It squeaks like a mouse. It whirrs and thrums and squeaks and squeals then turns a somersault. Now his brain is silent. His head aches. Now the sounds start up again like a million blacksmiths hammering a million anvils. He observes each blacksmith in turn. Some are white, some are black. There is a pattern to it he cannot understand. The pattern, that is. He cannot understand the pattern. Now

The Man by the Lake

every second blacksmith is smiling at him, beckoning to him. Is it his head they want upon their anvils?

His head upon their anvils. He imagines it now. No sooner has he imagined it than it is there, his head upon an anvil. And a blacksmith beating it with a rubber mallet. That, he assumes, his head may not split too soon, too soon would be too soon, though what is too soon? Soon enough? Not soon enough? Soon anyway. Soon his head will split from the hammering upon the anvil (they are lining up, these blacksmiths, black and white, hammering in turn) but not yet. Not yet. The beating becomes more rhythmical. Like African drums. He imagines African drummers dressed in colourful robes in a clearing on the savannah banging drums. All day long they bang in unison not stopping. Not stopping even for a tea break. Do they drink tea in Africa? Or a fag break. Do they smoke fags in Africa? No, they smoke grasses and herbs. Not even that. Not for anything do they stop. A lion comes prowling from the savannah, sniffs round them and leaves. Still they drum. The sun goes cartwheeling away to the west, dusk appears, bats fly about, do they have bats in Africa, still they drum. In fact their drumming intensifies. Where you might expect it to stop or at least slacken it intensifies. Faster, pounding, louder. Louder and louder. Ha ha, he thinks. Yes, excellent.

The boy's mouth is opening and closing. The girl comes back with a tray of drinks.

Drink, papa? she says, smiling sweetly.

Drink papa? O yes that's a good one. I'm not falling for that, he thinks.

Drink, mama?

O yes darling, thank you. Just a little one. Or maybe not such a little one.

The girl eyes him as she pours her mama's drink. No, he thinks, not this time.

Still the boy yaps away in silence. Who is this boy? he wonders.

He is connected to some sort of machine and doctors in white coats busy themselves around him. White coats, protective glasses, surgical masks, clipboards. Like an array of ghosts. Are you ghosts? he says in his normal voice. The nearest doctor jumps two feet in the air. He's fading fast, he says returning to dry land, though his voice, muffled by his mask, is almost inaudible. But still, he thinks, not as inaudible as the boy's. The boy is speaking perfectly normally; now his brow furrows and he runs his fingers through his hair. His features darken and he points a finger angrily at him. Has he done something wrong? Ah, yes, he thinks, wrong. Yes, that's it. All the things I've done wrong. I have done wrong to the boy and the girl and the woman. The girl and the woman do not seem to mind. Perhaps they do. The girl looks at him and gives him a sly smile. You are my daughter, I am your papa, are you flirting with me? No, she says, not flirting. Measuring. Measuring? Yes, you need to be measured. For your funeral clothes. My funeral clothes? Your funeral clothes. We're going to lay you out in the front room, O you'll look splendid. People will come from miles around. They will gather, there, in the front room, to see you off. It will be like your birthday and Christmas rolled into one. But I don't want to die! O don't be silly, we all have to die. You especially. You're first. You're the nasty one. Me, the nasty one? Do you really not know?

He's reviving, says the masked doctor and writes down something on his clipboard.

Interesting, very interesting, says the second doctor.

Very very interesting, says the third doctor, a woman.

Now all three doctors approach and peer at him from close range.

Bleeding on the brain? says the woman doctor.

Normal to have a little bleeding *in situ*, says the first doctor.

But not him, says the second doctor.

Why not? says the woman doctor.

The boy is becoming angrier and angrier. Now he is shaking his fist at him. He is grabbing him by the lapels. The girl gives him

The Man by the Lake

a sidelong look as if to say, Well, you asked for it. I don't believe I did, he says. The girl doesn't appear to hear him. The woman feeds the dog. The dog yaps soundlessly. I know, he thinks, I need to adjust the volume. At the end of the table is an audio console with various levers. He moves the levers up and down. Now the dog's yaps are clearly audible, now birdsong, now the tormenting girl who claims to be his daughter, now the singing birds. Finally the boy. Though is he a boy? He towers over him. Not so much a boy as a young man. Hello young man, he says, thinking to appeal to his vanity. It does no good. The boy is hurling abuse at him, terrible vile abuse, abuse strung together with swear words such that he has never heard. He glances across to the woman who continues to feed the dog oblivious to the boy's foul-mouthed diatribe. The girl begins to dance, a seductive dance around a flower-bedecked maypole that involves her slowly removing her clothes. But you are my daughter! Not any more. On she dances, swaying, teasing, letting her clothes slip to the ground one by one. He feels himself becoming aroused.

Good. Excellent, says the woman doctor.

Very good, purrs the first doctor.

Arousal, says the woman doctor.

At last, says the second doctor.

I thought it would never happen, says the woman doctor.

Nor I, says the second doctor.

Now the doctors too begin to dance, the woman leading, discarding her clipboard, her protective glasses, her gown. Not yet, he notices, her mask. The male doctors jiggle fiercely up and down on the spot as though unsure how far they should go. The woman doctor has no such inhibitions. Beneath her gown she is wearing a green top and mauve Hawaiian-style skirt. Off they come. She is wearing pink underwear with tassels on the tips of her bra. Round and round they whirl. Up and down go the male doctors. Stop! he cries. No-one pays any attention.

On and on the drummers drum. Lions circle them and slowly other creatures of the savannah appear: giraffes, elephants, snakes,

Dreams and Deceptions

crocodiles, antelopes, hippopotami. Am I a hippopotamus? he wonders. Perhaps I am. Perhaps, when all meaning is revealed, it will turn out that I was not I but instead a hippopotamus. Do we know what we are? We do not. We know only what we think we are. Therefore we may as well be hippopotami. I may be a hippopotamus, he says.

The woman stops dancing. The men too.

What was that?

Did he speak?

They bend over him. The male doctors smell of nothing. The woman doctor smells of scent.

His sense of smell is returning, says the woman doctor.

His sense of smell, all will be well! sing the male doctors in unison.

Taste too perhaps, says the woman doctor, bending so close over him he can almost taste her.

Yes, his taste buds are activating, says the woman doctor.

He takes a dangling tassel in his mouth and pulls with his teeth.

O yes, says the woman, taste and smell! He's all a-go!

He's all a-go! sing the male doctors bending their knees before bouncing back up again.

Would you like a suck? says the woman doctor. She upends her arms behind her back and unclips her bra, removes it with one skilful movement and allows it to fall to the floor.

Vile fucking bastard! Worse than the fucking worms beneath my feet! shouts the boy. He is clearly agitated. What it is he sees in him he does not know. Something unpleasant. No, worse. Evil. Evil? What is evil? Something from the Bible, that old story, where some were branded good and some evil. Some evil. Evil: a sinner against God. He has not, not consciously, not intentionally, sinned against anyone, least of all God. He is actually as innocent as it is possible to be. He thought of nothing but himself. What could be more innocent than that? He never intended harm to anyone unless they got in his way.

But of course, he thinks with a sigh, they did get in his way. They all got in his way one way or another. The woman, the boy, the girl. He looks across at the woman while the boy continues his foul diatribe. She is behaving as if he wasn't there. That's interesting, he thinks. Would she be behaving any differently if this strange scene, the boy standing in front of him yelling obscenities at him, were not in fact happening?

Perhaps it is not in fact happening.

He retunes the dial. Now the boy falls silent (though still his mouth opens and shuts, still he points). The girl, bored of her dance now that nobody is watching, picks up her clothes and walks sulkily back to the house. Now he hears only the woman. There's a boy! she is saying to the dog. Yap yap yap, says the dog. There's a boy! But now he sees she is not feeding him but teasing him – holding out a tempting biscuit than snatching it away as soon as the dog jumps for it. Each time the dog subsides, defeated, to his haunches. There's a *good* boy! She holds up another biscuit. Yap yap yap! Yap yap yap! Good boy! She holds the morsel

O for God's sake, give the bloody dog a biscuit!

What was that?

What was that? What was that? sing the doctors.

Have a suck, says the female doctor and carefully lowers her large dusky breast to his mouth (for she is, he notices now, not European but Asian). He grips the nipples with his teeth and sucks greedily. As greedily as though he were new-born baby. Am I a new-born baby? I cannot be, he thinks, I have all these memories. O memories, says the woman doctor, memories. They prove nothing. Suck. He sucks, feels the warm oozing substance enter his mouth and throat.

The substance enters his mouth and throat!

The substance enters his mouth and throat!

You can have all you want, says the woman doctor. Go on, have some more

Dreams and Deceptions

Bang bang bang, go the drums. The animals begin to dance. We are only here but for a short time, keep on drumming, the drums seem to say.

Drum drum drum. The day moves slowly into night and the animals wander away. To sleep, he thinks. To find some quiet spot to get their heads down before waking at sunrise and slaughtering each other all over again. Though do they sleep? Not all of them. Some take advantage of the night to steal a march on the others. While the others sleep some, the cats for example, go on night patrols. Prowling, looking for weak spots in their enemies' defences. Though are prey enemies? The predator and the prey, are they enemies? Most of the time they are not; it is only when the predator becomes hungry that the question even arises. The prey are happier than the predators, he thinks. They live quite peacefully without this disturbance of hunger. They graze the plain and feel no fear until the predators start prowling; then they run or huddle in groups hoping the predator will pick not them but some other, a cousin or a sister. Then, when the picking is done, they return to their peaceful grazing. We can endure almost any loss, he thinks, except the loss of self.

We can endure almost any loss except the loss of self! sing the doctors, clapping their hands to their foreheads.

The woman doctor is becoming more intimate, as if she is gaining some sort of sexual charge from his greedy sucking. Mmm, she is saying, that's nice, that is nice

That's nice! That is nice! sing the doctors, throwing their arms skywards and smiling broadly.

Can I slip in with you? Mmm, yes. She wriggles off her pink panties and climbs onto the platform upon which he is stationed. We are going to try a little experiment, she says. It's called 'erection'.

Erection! Erection!

He feels his prick stiffening; yet when he reaches down he finds he has no hands and no prick either.

Don't worry, sex is all in the mind, says the woman doctor.

The Man by the Lake

You are the one for me.
The one for me! A nice cup of tea!
What about them?
What about who?
The dancing doctors.
O don't worry about them. They're just monitoring the situation. Taking notes.
Notes?
Notes! Notes!
Yes, notes, we have to take notes. Otherwise we wouldn't be doctors.
Are you a doctor?
No, not really. She is making herself comfortable, stretching out beside him, rubbing herself against him. She leans closer and sticks her tongue into his mouth. He sucks on it as once, a child with his mama, he sucked on a lollipop.
Nice, he says.
Isn't it nice?
Nice! Nice!
It is nice, he says. It reminds me, when I was a child – am I boring you?
Not at all. I'm all ears.
Are you?
Not really. It just means I'm listening.
Will the drums ever fall silent? He doubts it. The animals are sleeping, except for the prowling cats, but the drums bang on. Bang bang bang. Bangbangbang. Bangbang bang bang, bang bang bang bang. So many of them. From at first just three or four now there are hundreds of drummers, all dressed in colourful robes, stretching as far as the eye can see.
The eye can see! The eye can see!
Some old some young some thin some fat, some bald, some with dreadlocks down to their waists.
Do you hear them? he asks the woman doctor.
Hear what darling?

Dreams and Deceptions

The drummers.

The woman doctor frowns and cocks an ear.

No, I don't think so. Drummers?

Yes, hundreds of them. Loud. Very loud. Very very loud. Drowning out even the blacksmiths' hammering.

No, she says, I still don't hear them.

No, she says, she doesn't hear them!

I've been looking for someone like you all my life.

Someone like me? he says.

Now at last the boy falls silent, all passion spent. And passion does spend itself and the end does come. That young man's anger couldn't last for ever. Nothing lasts for ever, not even anger. How angry he was. How angry I once was. How angry. And my anger visited upon those who were in my way. Almost everyone was in my way.

Almost everyone was in his way! sing the doctors, sinking to their knees.

I hope I'm not in your way. Am I in your way? says the woman doctor.

You are the way.

You're a gentleman.

Am I?

Hmm. Maybe not. Sometimes.

Most of the time?

Perhaps not even that. But sometimes.

Sometimes!

Can I collate those times, the times I was, and get rid of the rest?

Can I collate those times and get rid of the rest! sing the doctors, bouncing on the soles of their feet and flinging open their arms.

Memory is selective, says the woman doctor, sticking her tongue in his mouth. As though to shut him up, he thinks. He feels himself stiffening again. Will he, he thinks, actually make love to this very obliging woman doctor in full view of the dancing

The Man by the Lake

doctors? Good, good, he hears her say, kissing him. Will she have his baby?

Good boy! says the woman as the dog waits, lifting the biscuit high above his head. Good *good* boy! The dog jumps, cannot quite reach the biscuit, falls back with a yelp. Good good boy! She holds up the biscuit again, just out of the dog's reach.

Now the girl is tidying away the empty plates and glasses from the table. The boy is sitting on a low bank strumming a guitar.

A man and a woman appear from the French windows that overlook the garden. The woman has a small dog on a lead. They stand on the terrace and look down at the guitar-strumming boy. The boy pays them no attention, does not, in fact, appear to be aware of their presence. He is strumming his guitar quite fiercely and wailing in a strange manner, his face contorting, twisting his neck and looking up as though singing to the sky. O bright star look down on me! he cries loudly though there are no stars, bright or otherwise, to be seen. Cast petals on my bayaybee! Petals? How can stars cast petals? I am alone on the deep dark sea! No idea, he thinks disapprovingly. What is this foolish young man singing about? Does he not know where he is? The only number is number three

Number three. Now he's talking. Threesomes. Trinities. There's a lot to be said for the number three. Man and woman and bayaybee. Man woman and, for that matter, guitar strumming youth. A man and two women. Father, son and holy ghost. Three – aha! – doctors. Three doctors, two male, one female. Is that not always the case? Do doctors not always come in threes? No, that's disasters

The lights in the harbour!
(Yes, the ships at sea)
Don't shine on me!

Why not, he thinks, they shine quite randomly. There are no respecters of persons. They are not even animate. Though, he

Dreams and Deceptions

supposes, in another sense light is always animate. What is the universe made of?

I'm like a lost ship

O no, he thinks, here we go again. Why are long-haired guitar-strumming youths always lost?

Out there on the sea

The man takes a cigarette from a silver cigarette case, places it between his lips and lights it with an old-fashioned lighter. The woman takes his arm. Isn't it appalling? she says.

Yes, says the man, blowing out smoke and gazing ruminatively into the distance.

We might all be dead within a week.

Probably will be.

No sooner have they spoken than, as though reading their minds, an aeroplane appears, flying low over the trees that surround the house, and starts strafing them gunfire. No-one moves. The guitar player wails, the dog bounces around his mistress's ankles yapping, the man smokes and gazes into the distance, the woman holds his arm and looks into his face.

Did you say goodbye to Aunt Hilda?

No. Did you?

No.

Well then.

Yes, well then.

The woman turns her attention to the dog. She takes a biscuit from the pocket of her coat and holds it just out of the dog's reach. The dog jumps and misses, falls yelping to the ground.

O for god's sake give the damn dog a biscuit, says the man.

He has to be taught.

Taught what?

Life is not a piece of cake.

Would you like me to suck you? says the woman doctor. His prick is stiff yet he cannot locate it, nor those places in the woman where he might, if he could find it, insert it.

The Man by the Lake

O yes please.
Would you like me to suck you? O yes please! sing the doctors, bobbing up and down and throwing their arms about.
The woman doctor's head disappears from view. He feels nothing for a while, then, as if by magic, the feel of lips upon his prick. Lips upon my prick! he gasps.
Lips upon his prick! Lips upon his prick!
Mmm, says the woman doctor, desisting from her sucking for a moment. Is that nice?
Is that nice? Is that nice?
Yes, he says, very. Keep going.
Mmm, says the woman doctor, returning to his prick.
Mmm!!! Mmm!!!
He is about to ejaculate but then he thinks: best not. Perhaps the woman doctor would not like his ejaculation in her mouth. Ejaculation, he thinks, should be reserved for other places. One of the woman's other holes.
One of the woman's other holes!
Do you love me? says the woman doctor, resurfacing.

And as for this young man, what is the point of him? says the man, when the aeroplane has banked, turned and disappeared back whence it came.
Good question, says the woman.
A question to which there is no answer, says the man.
The very best sort of question, says the woman.
Miss you bayaybee, you know I do!
Not what's he on about?
O pretty baby I'll always be true!
Just feeling his way, says the woman.
As we once felt ours, says the man.
Did we? says the woman.
O I think so, says the man, tipping ash upon the terrace paving. My way or the highway.
The highway always seemed the better option, says the woman.

Dreams and Deceptions

But was it really an option? says the man.

Yap yap yap, says the dog. The man aims a kick at its ribs but it darts away and hides behind the woman's skirt.

Do you remember our first baby? says the man.

Dimly, says the woman. We weren't speaking, remember?

Nor we were, says the man.

The boy puts down his guitar and takes from his pocket a long thin cigarette paper and some tobacco. He sprinkles tobacco upon the paper, adds some weed, rolls it into a cigarette. He inserts a rolled up edge of cardboard into one end, sets fire to it and smokes. Halfway through the cigarette he keels over onto his side and lies staring up at the sky.

They'll be back, says the woman.

I dare say they will.

The woman sighs. Aren't they always?

And on it goes, says the man. God knows why.

We certainly don't, says the woman.

The girl appears from inside the house and stands beside the man and the woman. She looks down at the glassy-eyed boy.

What's wrong with him?

O, the usual, says the woman.

Not again.

Yes, again.

Will he never learn?

Probably not.

I've been on this earth for fifty-five years, says the man. Fifty-five, a good age, don't you think?

A bloody ridiculous age, says the girl, going back inside the house.

I wish we had some servants, says the woman. To attend to our needs. Instead of having to do everything ourselves.

The servants have all run away, says the man.

Would you like to father my baby? Only I've asked and asked

The Man by the Lake

and hunted around and can't find anyone willing to take it on, says the woman doctor.

O yes, he says.

Are you sure? It's a big responsibility.

I don't mind.

But are you sure? I mean, I wouldn't want to get into this, go through with it so to speak, only to find at the end of the day you were not a good father.

I was a very good father, he says indignantly. A very good father indeed.

Did your children love you?

I think so. They went their own way in the end. They always do.

Do they? says the woman doctor.

The girl reappears on the terrace with a tray carrying three glasses, a bottle of gin, a bottle of chilled tonic water and a plate of sliced lemons. She places the tray on a green metal lattice-work table and pours three drinks, one for her mama, one for her papa and one for herself. They raise their glasses.

To the good times! says the man.

The good times! echo the woman and the girl.

The good times, he says. Those were the days.

Were there many good times? says the woman doctor.

Good times! Good times! sing the doctors, tearing off their masks and flinging them into the air.

Very few, as far as I recall, he says.

Now the blacksmiths are back, one two three. Four five six. All dressed like doctors in white gowns and surgical masks. Bang bang bang. One in particular looms in and out of his vision – a great bearded brute of a man with an unholy grin and blood on his teeth. Lay your head upon the altar! sing the doctors. And if you do you didn't oughta! He lays his head upon the blacksmith's anvil. The position is not quite right. The blacksmith manoeuvres

Dreams and Deceptions

him this way and that but still the position is not quite right. Let him sleep, says the woman doctor. It's been quite a strain for him. Strain is good, says the first doctor. Very good, says the second doctor. Like a stress test. To see if he's fit. Is he fit? says the woman doctor, replacing her bra over her large dusky breasts and angling her arms behind to clip the straps together. Hard to tell at this stage, says the first doctor. We can only wait and see. A bit of a disappointment, so far, wouldn't you say? A disappointment yes but there's always time, says the woman doctor.

Bang bang bang go the drums. No-one moves.
    The long-haired boy yawns and sits up.
    I've had the most extraordinary dream, he says. Unfortunately I can't remember what it was.
    You and your dreams, says the girl, who is sitting on the bank beside him constructing a daisy chain.
    I saw the holy trinity then a great explosion. And out of the explosion came
    Yes? says the girl, threading the daisy chain into her hair and turning to look at him.
    Mice.
    Mice?
    Hundreds, thousands, of white mice. With pink noses and pink feet. Why do you suppose their feet and noses are pink?
    Because they're in the pink, says the girl.
    Like us, says the long-haired boy. Pink.
    Careful, says the girl.
    The aeroplane returns, winging low over the trees, angling towards them. And a second plane coming in from another direction. A pincer movement. Why, he wonders, when they are already sitting ducks? The boy and girl do not move, just glance up as the garden is strafed with machine gun fire. None of the bullets hits them or appears to do any damage at all.
    That was a near miss, says the boy.
    Was it? says the girl. Perhaps it wasn't.

The Man by the Lake

    No, perhaps it wasn't. Would you like to hear my new song?
    No, thank you, says the girl.

    A spoonful of sugar makes the medicine go down.
    A spoonful of sugar makes the medicine go down!
    I do not wish to sleep. Let me be clearer. I do wish to sleep but at the same time I do not wish to sleep. Lest I not awake.
    O, you will wake, says the woman doctor. One way or another.
    What way might that be?
    The one and only way. There is only one way.
    Only one wayyy! sing the doctors.
    Why do they keep singing? he asks the woman doctor.
    They love to sing. Boys will be boys.
    We love to sing! Boys will be boys!
    Is everything a song?
    I don't think so. Now rest. You need some rest. You're not yourself today.

The boy takes the girl in his arms. She resists but perfunctorily as though resistance were useless. The sun is shining and the world is at peace. From time to time the planes fly over, as if in mute reproach, but no longer strafe them with bullets. Or what he assumed were bullets: perhaps they were not bullets. The man and woman stand on the terrace with their cocktails gazing gloomily towards the wood while the boy and the girl make love on the bank below them. When I was their age I never did it in public, says the woman. I had more decorum. *Decorum est pro patria mori*, says the man. In summers then. Will they have a baby, do you suppose? Birds sing in the trees as though to sing the world into being. I don't think so, says the man.

Bang bang bang bang bang. The whole savannah is alive with drummers, hundreds, thousands of them, stretching as far as the lake's edge. The lake itself is as wide as a sea, stretching from one end of the horizon to the other, and alive with flamingoes, ungainly birds, tall as telegraph poles, pink and one-legged, craning their necks to delve in the water with their huge beaks. Bang bang bang bang bangetty bang: standing, sticks whirling, sitting, crouching, kneeling, their eyes glazed over with the rhythm until it seems their arms and hands are drumming quite independently of any intent.

Quite independently of any intent!

Quite independently of any intent!

The animals stand nonplussed staring of the drummers. Will they ever cease? Will they ever vanish?

The girl kisses the boy. Thank you, she says, that was nice.

Glad I could be of service.

O I wouldn't call it that, says the girl.

What would you call it?

The girl rises, walks past the man and the woman, who pay no attention to her, and re-enters the house. Birds sing in the trees as though without the song, without the naming, there would be no world. There would be no world, he thinks, unless we relentlessly summon it into being. Only when our eyes droop does the world cease to exist. What was it Bishop Berkeley said? He was a bishop after all, he must have been right. Something about palm trees and desert islands. Are we on an island?

Yes, we're on an island! Yes, we're on an island!

The woman doctor leans over him and kisses him on the lips. Her lips are soft and warm and surprisingly fragrant, as though she has re-fragranced herself in the interim. The garden is beautiful, he thinks, so peaceful, though just at that moment the aeroplanes reappear, a whole squadron of them this time, ripping up the ground with streams of bullets, their bullets cutting strange patterns and shapes in the ground, flinging earth up and out in every direction. The boy does not move as the bullets rip up the ground beside him. The man and the woman also do not move, although, after a while, as bullets tear into the fabric of the house, they begin to dance. An awkward shuffle at first, his arm around her waist, as though they have not danced for a long time; but slowly their steps become more fluent and their bodies attune. The world is called into being, he thinks, and yet we are not in it. The doctors busy themselves with their clipboards, jotting down notes, occasionally looking up, but at each other not at him, as though he wasn't there.

Night

You lift up your arms, lift them straight up above your head, and yet you are asleep. Light is creeping through the window, light and the sound of jackdaws, and your arms are raised above your head and you are talking in your sleep.
    No, you cry, get off!
    Mumble mumble mumble.
    Gerroff!
    What is it babe?
    You open your eyes (your arms still lifted straight up) and look at me. O, you say, and close your eyes again.
    Babe? Are you okay?
    Yes. No.
    You open your eyes. Sunlight is streaming through the window and I remember the sun when I was a child in my grandmother's house, watching the dustmotes spinning in the light beams.
    I was being chased by big hairy monsters.
    Who?
    My sisters.
    Your sisters?
    But you are asleep again and your arms descend, slowly and gracefully, until they lie, neatly folded, across your chest.
    Which sisters, babe?
    You are snoring now, snoring through your teeth, your mouth slack and your teeth rattling together. I try to switch you round, propel you onto your side.
    Gerroff! Gerroff!
    It's okay, babe, it's me. You're snoring.
    And now you're conversing with your sisters and I can only

Night

catch the odd word...Mr Shutler...Gerroff!...No I won't, Panda!... Gerroff!...I put it there...I put the packet there, it was only a small packet...Gerroff!...It was there...
    You open your eyes.
    O, you say, I was dreaming about my sister.
    Your good sister or your bad sister?
    Panda. I was fighting with Panda.
    Were you a child?
    I don't know.
    The light is flooding through the window now, through the thin curtain. I lean over and kiss your dry lips.
    I have to go, today.
    You have to go?
    Yes. Just for a few days.
    O don't go. You put your arms round me, pull me tight. Don't go.
    I feel my senses rising, I want you, and yet I do nothing.

    What is your earliest memory?
    You laugh. Why?
    I just want to know all about you. I love you, babe.
    You put your mouth up to mine.
    Well?
    Well what?
    What is your earliest memory?
    O, I don't know. My mum I guess.
    Doing what? What was your mum doing?
    I don't know!
    You laugh and pull me closer.
    You must remember something.
    Okay. I remember Panda stamping on my head.
    Stamping on your head?
    She was always a vicious beast, Panda.
    Why?
    I don't know. She just was.

Dreams and Deceptions

Worse than Carly?
Yes, probably. I don't know. Don't go.
I have to go. You know I do. I told you. I explained. I'll be back in three days, maybe four.
I don't want you to go. I'm scared.
Scared of what?
I don't know. Just scared.
There's nothing to be scared of here. It's the safest place in the world.
It's not. It's not safe.
It is. Besides, you can go and see Jean. Go to Pilates class.
I don't want to go to Pilates class.
You've got your drawing set. Have you started using it yet?
No. I'm scared, babe.
So what did Panda do?

You close your eyes and pull me closer and for a moment you are asleep again, your mouth trembling, your body shaking. Your fingers clutching at my chest, scratching, as though to scratch out the devil from your dreams. The light filters through the translucent curtain and beyond the curtain the shapes of the trees in the castle grounds are visible, and inside the trees the endless crying and cawing of the rooks and jackdaws. They have been there, it would seem, since the dawn of time, and yet they, like us, are new. In dreams we become ourselves. You are always dreaming, your sleep is filled with dreams and when you wake you cling to your dreams and will them not to disappear, for in your dreams you are born again.

You open your eyes and say,
I love waking up with you.
I know, babe.
Kiss me.
I kiss you and you fall asleep again, muttering and mumbling. Gerroff!...Panda!...
It is when we are closest to what we are.
And what are we?

Night

Now you are shuddering and kicking, moaning, and suddenly you lash out with your coiled fist and punch me in the eye.
I clap my hand to my face.
Babe!
You open your eyes and look at me.
What happened?
You punched me!
O no, did I? You start to laugh. I'm sorry. I thought I was punching Panda.
Did you have any good times when you were a child?
Yes. No.
You turn round, turn towards the grey light that comes seeping through the thin blue curtain of our room, pull the covers over your head. Curl around me.
I don't know. I don't think so. Maybe.
It can't have been all bad.
It wasn't.
Now you are asleep again, untroubled as a child. I think, It is all two people who fall in love can do, help ease the pain. All else is vanity.

I rise, slip from the bed, pad along the passage to the kitchen. Flick the kettle on, pad silently next door and find a CD to play. Stand and stare at the flickering TV. On the tilt-top table an overflowing ashtray and two empty bottles of wine. Wine splashed on the carpet red as blood.
The music plays softly, the guitars whine with a trembling beauty. I make my way silently along the passage to the bathroom and there you are, shattered and shuttered, lying quite still in the bath and your eyes turn slowly and look into mine. I think, It used to be easy to make love then, when everything was ahead of you. All love, all passion…now every moment is filled with meaning and filled with dread.

Horses

Marcus comes thumping up the stairs with Caitlin. They are arguing. I am in my bedroom sorting out bits of hi-fi. I have a woman coming round tomorrow to buy the Ravensbourne – tonight, I plan to rig it up for a last night of pleasurable listening. I will listen to something that really turns me on – Horses by Patti Smith, maybe.

My door is open. As they reach the landing, Caitlin's eye alights upon me.

She wanders in and sits down. Marcus goes thumping on up before realising Caitlin has abandoned him.

How are you, Caitlin?

Fine. And yourself?

I'm okay. Just sorting out some hi-fi stuff.

You and your hi-fi stuff.

You know me.

I do not.

I look at Caitlin. I'd always thought her pretty despite her sticking-out teeth: black hair, blue eyes, orange freckles, red lips. A pretty face and a nice body, too.

She is ensconced now, sitting on the floor with her back to the wall.

Well maybe you should.

Maybe I should. What are we having on?

Patti Smith. Do you like Patti Smith?

Caitlin looks doubtful. It isn't the sort of music she knows. She just knows the obvious stuff – Donna Summer, Abba, the Eagles.

Do you not have the Eagles?

Do I not have them? What sort of question is that?

Horses

It's my question is what sort of question it is.

Well the answer to your question, Caitlin, is, Yes. Yes, I do not have them.

There you go again. Trying to trick me.

Why would I want to trick you?

To get into my panties.

Why would I want to get into your panties?

Caitlin smiles a slow, lascivious smile. Her sticking-out teeth actually seem to enhance her attractiveness.

Everyone else does. Is it that you do not?

Marcus's voice wafts down from above. He is asking Caitlin to come up. He is running two women this week – a rather plain English one and this piece of unmistakable Irish talent. I know which one I'd go for, any day. Not that I'd made any sort of move.

Come up, he calls down.

I look at Caitlin. She lifts her eyebrows.

He can want.

Sounds like he does.

How about you?

How about me what?

Do you want?

Do I want what, Caitlin?

To get inside my panties.

Okay.

Okay? What sort of answer is that? I want someone who'll wine and dine me. Take me out. Make me feel like a lady.

Caitlin, I almost say, you must be joking. It'll take more than an Aberdeen Angus steakhouse and bottle of burgundy to make a lady out of you.

Instead I say,

Have a listen. Maybe you will.

Will what?

Like it.

And I put on 'Horses'.

Dreams and Deceptions

Caitlin is enraptured right away.

Jeez, this is good, she says, closing her eyes and leaning her head against the wall. She is actually rather beautiful, leaning there like that. Her face is the right shape, everything fits fine. There's something off-putting about her though. It's the combination of her sticking out teeth and her boldness.

Jesus died for somebody's sins – but not mine, sings Patti.

That's just how I feel, says Caitlin.

Mary Mary Quite Contrary

What happened next?
I don't remember. I only remember the child sharks dolphin fish birds gathered round him. Were they protecting him? If so, from what?
What happened next?
I don't remember. They said, Whose is this child, this unprotected child with fish and birds gathered round him in the sparkling sunlight, I don't remember. Whose is this child?
And then, what then?
I don't remember. The child was weeping no not weeping laughing his cheeks blown out was he a trumpeter perhaps yes a trumpeter but if he were a trumpeter was he a trumpeter?
And after that?
The fish and birds were gone. They flew away perhaps at least were gone. The fish the birds were gone. Flown. The doors as it were shut. Who remembers that? Only those who weren't there.
What time of day was this judged by the sun?
There was not. Not in the manner of which you speak   nor the flesh corrupt and bloodied. But I saw him.
What happened next?
The child was laughing and the seas rolled over him he was gone.
But he returned?
The seas parted. The day was cloudless. High above the highest mountain there was cloud and between the blue of the sky and the white cloud ten birds flew I counted them on the fingers of my hands.
What happened next?
I said, Whose is this child? Why is he here?

Dreams and Deceptions

We took a boat, Mary and I. At first the captain did not want to let us embark. There is no room, he said. See? And he pointed towards the open deck where a dozen or more passengers were gathered. It's full. I'm only allowed sixteen. I counted them and there were fifteen not including the captain. There are only fifteen, I said. He sighed. Very well, he said. But only one on deck and the other with me in the cabin. The day was beautiful, I said, Such a day we may never see again. We cast off. He turned the boat and a gull came, one of those great black things with red on its bill but it was not white and black but brown and could not fly it sat at the far end and then out of nowhere a wind came up. Could be a rocky ride, said the captain. But the day, I said. O yes, this of all days, he muttered, his expression quite sour. But you are the captain. That I am not, he said, and we cast off.

But if not he, who?

I put my arm around Mary and steered her into the cabin to protect her from the wind, she had no coat but only a shawl about her shoulders. But no, she said, I want to stay with you. But the captain, I said, and the wind. No, she said, I want to stay with you.

In the still moment between life and death when everything stills, when all motion stops, how is it we cannot know. Enough of us have died and two at least come back. But even the second of the two said little of where he had been. He ascended into heaven. He came back to tell us all was well. We could die and come back.

Mary, Mary quite contrary   casts off her shawl quite angrily. You have brought me here to sail upon the blue ocean with a captain who is no captain and a crew who are no crew but rather fifteen faceless ones

We walked towards the mountain past two houses, Mary with her shawl around her head to protect her from the wind. A dog came

Mary Mary Quite Contrary

to the gate of the second house to bark at Mary. A woman came behind the dog.

He doesn't know you, she said. Who are you?

I'm Joe, I said. And this is Mary.

Are you walking across the mountain? Why not take the boat? said she.

We approached the captain but he told us there was no room.

He'll take anyone if you give him enough – the woman stopped speaking for a moment and rubbed the middle finger of her right hand against her thumb. Shekels.

We have no shekels, I said.

The woman became angry.

You have no shekels? Then what makes you think that you can ascend the mountain? Or indeed that anyone would want you to?

We are not beholden to you, I said.

You are on my land, said the woman.

So?

We do not want strangers round here.

We are not strangers.

You said your name was Joe and hers was Mary. You are strangers.

We are not strangers.

I will let you pass, said the woman. But once you have passed you cannot return.

Once we have passed we will not want to return, I said.

The day was cold, much colder than we had expected. Mary pulled her shawl around her. I carried no more than a single pack upon my back. It was all we possessed. We walked silently for two hours and the sun was at the zenith but still the day felt cold. For two hours we saw no-one, only the host of black birds that drifted above the mountain-top. A man and a woman were walking towards us, the man some way ahead of the woman. A stocky man with curly hair and brown trousers tied with a belt. The man carried a gun and stopped before us.

Dreams and Deceptions

Your names, he said, curtly.

We are not beholden to you, I replied.

Then to whom? he said and laughed, showing an array of misshapen, darkened teeth.

I said nothing.

The woman caught up with the man and slipped her arm through his.

Strangers, he said.

Not strangers, said the woman, peering intently. I have seen them before.

Where?

I cannot place them.

So, said the man.

We come in peace, I said.

That's what they all say, said the man, unslinging his gun. Mary pressed herself to me. I raised my hand in a sign of peace and blessed the pair of them.

The day was clear but the air cold. We walked through a forest of pines, breathing in the sweet smell of the pine-cones. Red squirrels darted up the tree trunks pausing when they reached the higher branches to look back at us. Birds sang and one bird, a small bird with a curved bill, flew down almost to our feet before ascending in a spiral. The tree leaned in towards us as though it could not bear the weight of its branches.

Mary stopped.

When will we be there?

Soon.

And then?

And then?

What happens then?

Then we will be there.

I need to rest.

We continued through the forest until there was light, a tunnel of light, expanding as we walked towards it, as though drawing us in. Mary slipped her arm into mine but did not speak. We walked into the tunnel of light and beyond the tunnel of light, stark against the sky, we saw the mountain. Do we have eyes to see? We looked and it was there; we looked a second time and it was gone.

We walked along the edge of farmland. A dog joined us, a small farm dog, wagging its tail and drawing back the edges of its mouth in greeting. This dog will lead us to a place of sanctuary. We walked in single file behind the dog, the dog turning from time to time to ensure that we were following, along the edge of the farmland, onto the slopes of a hill and along a narrow track. As we rounded a curve in the track we saw before us, nestling on the slopes of the hill and looking back towards the sea, a house the size of six houses, built of granite and stone. A house the size of six houses built of granite and stone with windows the size of walls but no glass in them and half the roof missing trees and plants growing and the wind whistling through the empty windows. A house abandoned. The dog led us and we came to lawns unkempt and overgrown and terraces as empty and silent as the house itself. A mansion, or what had once been a mansion. Built for God knows whom God knows when. Left to fall into ruin until it is gone, abandoned, at one with the mountainside, swallowed up by wind and sand and time.

We will rest here, I said.
In this God-forsaken place?
The dog led us here.
The dog led us?
But now standing waiting at the entrance to the house, below ground level, where the ground sloped down to an entrance of stone with no door and no shelter from wind or rain, where nothing lived but bats and birds and other creatures   we stood and stared and looked around us.

Dreams and Deceptions

Sometimes in dreams we think we are other. Sometimes in dreams we are other.
 The child is not yours, she said.
 I wondered then as the dog ran around us snapping at gnats caught on the sea breeze the way a dog might jump for a rubber ball the way dogs jump and play or box each others' ears. But this dog, this little blue merle, had no others' ears to box. Playing in the sun or eating daisies he was content to follow us did he ask nothing from God.
 Then whose? I said.
 That night we built a fire for the night was cold. We had expected cold but not the bitter cold that encircled the house and slid into our bones. We huddled together, Mary and I, seeking each other's warmth, before the day came. When without thinking I slid my arms round her   she pushed me away.
 I rose at first light and gathered wood for the fire. The dog lay flat to the ground watching me with dark eyes. When the fire came up he began to bark, running back and forth, lying flat to the ground, there was fear in his eyes. I am a sailor, I said, I have walked upon the water. The fire came up and soon the wood was burning, cracking and spitting, and the heat rising. Today, I said, we will go on. Yet we did not.

After three days we went on by now Mary was heavy with child and the journey was an ordeal. Must we go on? she said, as she sank to her haunches beneath a dripping pine. We cannot stay, I said. And yet, she said, there are those who stayed. The wise ones. We are not wise ones, I said. The dog stayed with us then but by the evening of the fourth day he was gone.

Two strangers came amongst them, men with staves, but when they saw they were no threat, on the contrary, left them alone.

We walked for miles along a rough mountain track. Now, at midday, the sun was high and our clothes stuck to us like lemmings. Mary set her face and did not say another word. We came, that noon time, to a village. Men and women going about their daily toil, rising, raising, going down with the night. Every day the sun comes up to welcome us (or we to welcome it). The sun, then, is our only saviour. It brings heat and light. In the night we cannot see, only owls and foxes with their wide irises. But not in the blanket dark. In the dark there is nothing. In the dark you cannot see even yourself.

A man greeted us, a man six foot high with curly hair, I say a man though he was little more than a boy. Welcome, strangers, he said, do you seek a place to stay? We stay where we can, I said. Come, he said, I will take you to my mother's house, for Mary was heavy with child. We followed him through alleys made of mud and came to his mother's house. His mother sat with other women dressed in red, blue and gold. She rose to greet us, placing her hands to together as though in prayer. Welcome, she said softly. Have you travelled far? Come, she said, and prepared a place for us.

Have you thought of a name? she said to Mary. For the child I mean.

The name will come to us, I said.

But Mary said, A name has already come to me.

We slept that night in a stable with the warmth of the animals all around us. In the morning Mary was too sick to go on. You go on, she said; I will stay.

Dear Charlotte

My dear Charlotte, I am very much in love with you. But, and it's a big but, I do not wish in any way to curtail your freedom.
   Naj sucks the nib of his fountain pen and thinks.
   Freedom, he writes, is first and foremost. We are nothing if we are not free.
   Does he want Charlotte to be free?
   I have never – and here he pauses: the confession is almost too great to bear – been with woman.
   Woman? Or a woman?
   Women are not all the same despite their obvious similarities.

Dear Charlotte, he begins again. It was lovely seeing you and Jimmy the other day in the Pizza on the Park. Listening, some of the time, to jazz. And then and then
   And then. Food for thought. Sitting there, the three of them, two of them knowing what was going on and the other not. The other being him.
   And then
   He and Jimmy side by side pissing at the wall, and he saying, I'll run her home.
   And Jimmy saying, No, that's okay, I'll do it.
   No really, he persists. Foolishly as it turned out. With hindsight. Though how was he to know? And who was betraying whom? Was she betraying him? Was he betraying her?
   I will run her home, I always do, he says feebly.
   Except, says Jimmy, shaking the drops off the end of his cock, she isn't going home.

Dear Charlotte

Not going home. Still he didn't get it. If she wasn't going home where was she going? Out somewhere?

Not going home? he says stupidly.

That's right, says Jimmy, tucking his cock away.

And then the pair of them going back in and Charlotte nowhere to be seen.

They find her in the basement listening to jazz. Some sort of dinner jazz it sounds like. Some plump elderly coloured lady singing the blues to an accompaniment of piano, guitar and double bass. Charlotte sitting stock still, white as a feather, as though she'd seen a ghost.

Perhaps she had.

Perhaps he was a ghost.

O there you are, says Jimmy, peevishly.

Here I am, says Charlotte gravely.

And still, foolishly, he persists. She is not going home but she must be going somewhere. Perhaps he could come too?

Dear Charlotte, I am sorry for what happened the other night.

No that's not right. He sucks his pen. He isn't sorry. He didn't do anything. For what could he be sorry? It was she who betrayed him. She is the one who should be sorry.

That's not quite right either. She is the one who should be apologising. But apologising is not the same as being sorry.

Dear Charlotte, I am not sorry.

But he is sorry. Not for anything he did but for what happened. He is sorry it happened as it did. Perhaps he can wind back the clock and it will happen differently.

Dear Charlotte, I am so happy. So happy that we – that is, you and I – that we
    Finally
    After all these years
    You and I

Dreams and Deceptions

No it won't do. It isn't the truth. It didn't happen like that. And there is only one truth.

Dear Charlotte, l do not wish to curtail your freedom.
But curtailing Charlotte's freedom is exactly what he wishes to do.
Dear Charlotte, I
I
I
Love you. That's better. That's telling it like it is. That's the truth. But is it?

Dear Charlotte, I am very annoyed with you. We went to the Pizza in the Park, we met Jimmy, and the next thing
The next thing
The next fucking thing

Downstairs. Listening to dinner jazz. Some plump elderly coloured lady singing the blues. Quite famous apparently. They must have paid a lot to get her. Perhaps not. Perhaps singing the blues in the Pizza in the Park is so prestigious a gig they don't have to pay them anything. They must pay them something. Dear Charlotte

It's no good. He scrumples up the paper. He should ring her instead. Dear Charlotte. And she is dear to him, always has been. Dear Charlotte. She has had many lovers, he has had none. Perhaps that's what makes him stand out. Dear Charlotte, I am your humble servant. That's about right. He is her humble servant. Dear Charlotte, I would like to kill you. Better not say that, perhaps he will. Not a good look, a dead Charlotte and an incriminating letter in the same room. Dear Charlotte, I have killed you. I am your killer. I am the psycho-killer. Didn't you know? It was me all along. Dear Charlotte

Perhaps I don't love you any more.
Perhaps you never were the one for me.
Perhaps you are just a whore.
Dear Charlotte.

Jimmy tucks his cock away. He follows suit. He follows Jimmy down the stairs to the basement where a coloured lady is singing the blues. Strange fruit, something swinging in the trees. He doesn't get it. And Charlotte, pale as a ghost, sitting right beside the stage with her knees drawn up to her chin.

Would you like a lift home? he says.
Yes, thank you, says Charlotte.
Now it's Jimmy's turn to be annoyed.
But
O yes.
Charlotte seems undecided. So tiring having to decide. Instead she changes the subject.
Do you like this music? she says.
The singer drones on, her strange song about fruit.
Yes, he says.
No, says Jimmy.
No, neither do I. Not really, says Charlotte.
They make their way out and stand for a moment in the late evening London drizzle. Dear Charlotte, Jimmy and Naj.
Which way are you going? says Jimmy.
A flicker of a smile on Charlotte's ghostlike face.

Well, that was hard work, says Jimmy.
We shouldn't have just ghosted him like that.
Well he should have taken the hint.
He doesn't take hints, says Charlotte.
Why not? says Jimmy.
He just doesn't, says Charlotte.
Soon they are locked in an embrace upon the bed and Jimmy is

Dreams and Deceptions

entering her and looking down at her white face in the moonlight. She is, he thinks, one of the most beautiful women he has ever seen. She looks back though he cannot tell if she is looking at him or through him. She closes her eyes. He closes his and opens them. Hers are still closed. Dear Charlotte. What is she thinking now?

Dear Charlotte, what are you thinking now? writes Naj. Not that he has any right to know. He does not own her nor does he wish in any way to curtail her freedom.

Xeno

I crept late one night into Xeno's room and found him propped up in bed reading, his hand to his head, his cheeks flushed. He was wearing a pair of blue pyjamas.

He turned to me and smiled.

What are you reading?

He turned the cover: Japanese War Crimes by Lord Russell.

Look.

He opened the book to show me. The pictures were terrible beyond imagining: a man tied to a post with his eyes gouged out; a man torn limb from limb; a bound prisoner being used for bayonet practice. Mutilated corpses. Raped women. A man being buried alive.

The images stirred our blood. I sat on the bed, leaned down, brought my lips to his. He put one hand on the back of my head and pulled me onto him. I reached beneath the bedclothes, inside his pyjamas, found his cock. Felt him sigh and shudder.

I bit his lip and smiled.

You and I. Worse than them. Worse than the worst.

He was smiling coyly and I thought, not for the first time, how seductive he was. He was pretty and seductive as a girl.

I rose, untied my dressing gown, let it fall to the floor. As I pulled off my pyjamas he loosened and pushed down his. And the top, I said. His eyes held mine as his fingers went to the buttons and undid them. I slipped into the bed and pulled him to me; felt the warmth and softness of his naked flesh, the warmth and softness of his tongue.

I love you, I whispered.

Dreams and Deceptions

It was the last time we would make love. The last time we would ever even meet.

The book was fallen to the floor. We lay side by side, quite still. His eyes were closed. We sought what was real and true in love as we did in books. And yet our love was no more than a candle – a candle to keep the flame alive until the world changed.

I will always love you.

Only the silence of his breathing and the vacuum of his blue eyes.

No matter what happens. Whatever the life I lead or the death I die.

His silence was like an absence, a stillness at the very heart.

You as you are. Now exactly. Not as you will be or ever were.

His hand tightened on my breast and I heard him sigh. Felt him move; turn his face to the wall and fall into sleep. I rose within that starlit silence and pulled on my clothes. I turned to him one last time, bestowed one last kiss: bending, as a mother to kiss her child.

Goodbye, Xeno. You are, will always be, mine.

Love is merely a delusion, how often do we learn that. It is a delusion both ways: at the start or, if not then, by the end. Next day I left that place without a backward glance. I could not bear the life that had been mapped out for me – meetings, interrogations, form-filling, conforming to this or that. Playing a game I knew to be false. Instead I hitched a lift to London with another boy I knew, Edward Lanier, whose own beauty would, I hoped, help me to forget Xeno. We arrived at his father's house in Chelsea. His father, a wine merchant clad in a blue pin-stripe suit and polished leather shoes, stared at me.

What, he said, is your ambition?

I shrugged.

I don't think I have one.

Nothing?

No.
And your home, your family?
Dead. It was a lie, but an unimportant one.
All of them?
Mostly. I have an uncle somewhere but it's years since I've seen him. He was my father's elder brother but they had a falling out.
What became of your father?
My father was targeted at Roswell.
Roswell?
Yes. He was taken.
And your mother?
I sighed and lifted my eyes heavenward.
I am sorry you asked but as you have I must tell you the truth. My mother is alive but incarcerated in an establishment for the insane. Sometimes she knows me, sometimes she doesn't. She is unable to care for me at all.
Brothers, sisters? persisted the foolish merchant. It was the sort of interrogation I had fled to London to avoid. I looked at Edward, his fresh, smiling face, his big teeth, his big blue eyes, bigger and bluer even than Xeno's. I realised that though I might feast on his flesh like an anteater upon an anthill I could never love him. His large, white body would always be strange to me.
One of each, I said, rising. But both, like the others, gone.

I wandered the streets of Chelsea for two days and nights. I went back several times to the Laniers but they were always out, at least Edward and his father were. His mother came anxiously to the door, wiping her hands on a tea towel.
They are out.
Still out?
Yes. Could you come back later?
Could I wait?
O…She cast anxious glances hither and thither. O no. I too am about to go out. Come back later. They'll be back by six.

Dreams and Deceptions

I slid into a coffee bar like a fugitive and ordered a Coca Cola and a slice of chocolate cake. A girl came and sat in the neighbouring seat to mine. She was older than me by a year or two. She looked poised and confident, as though she knew her way around. She ordered *thé menthe* and produced a cigarette from her bag. I pulled a lighter from my pocket and clicked open the flame. She bent her head to inhale, glancing up at me with soft brown eyes as she did so.

Thank you.
My pleasure.
I haven't seen you here before?
I've only just arrived.
Where were you?
Out in –. I named the town but not the institution.
You are new to London?
Yes.
Do you have somewhere to stay?
I don't know.
You can stay with me.
Okay.

But first, there is something I want you to do for me. She delved in her pocket and produced a piece of paper with close writing on it. This is a prescription. Don't worry, it's all legal. Go across the road to the drugstore, get my prescription and bring it to me. Then I'll take you back to my place. You can stay as long as you like.

Okay, I said, and rose, her piece of paper in my hand. For the first time since I'd left Xeno my eyes were open to the new world and culture that surrounded me.

Anatolia

The van shudders over the Anatolian ghost roads.

Two dogs with golden fleeces running alongside a flock of sheep.

Men appearing and disappearing like archangels.

Sky as blue and permanent as the sea.

She is sitting beside him staring through the windscreen.

Now she is in the back with the children. Spooning food into their mouths, like a mother bird.

Mother bird = mother ship.

Sky as blue and permanent as the ghosts on the horizon.

The sun's rays stretch down remorselessly, like Jacob's ladder, like the tasselled bells on a dromedary.

Two dogs with golden fleeces

A man whistling on a hill somewhere (all history took place on this hill: stay here, stay still, do not wander, do not become a wanderer; all history, past, present and future, is here; there is no need to wander nor change; there is no need to go out into the world).

Music playing on a cassette: 'she rolls just like a river'

Last night they slept beneath Ararat. In the morning men with guns came to inspect the vehicle. Wandering round the vehicle, trying the doors. He leapt up, pulled on his pants, clambered into the front seat, fired up the engine before they could fire up him. What they would have done he doesn't know. She is in the back. Unblinking, staring not at him but at the children.

Are we nearly there?

That depends what nearly there means.

Dreams and Deceptions

'Nearly' or 'there'?

Either. Both. Nearly, therely. Near and there. Counterpoints

He hears the music of the heavens. It switches on, roars like Wagner, then switches off again.

Did you hear that?

Did I hear what?

The music...music of the heavens, I guess.

There is no music, James.

There was.

She smiles slightly. He knows that smile. It drives him mad.

There was, he says earnestly.

Well there isn't now, James.

There is...there! Did you hear it?

I didn't hear anything.

He knows she heard it. Her senses are more acute than his. Whatever he hears, she hears. And more. She hears everything. Hears things before they happen. Hears things that aren't there.

I know you heard it.

No, you don't.

Yes I do. I'm not stupid.

Her half smile.

I didn't say you were, she says.

He makes the front seat, fires up the engine, slams the van into gear. Drives. Expecting at any moment to hear the sound of gunshots. Over the rocky trails of the desert, slides into the road. Only one road. The long winding road through the mountains.

Only one road, he says.

Yes, she says. The long winding road through the mountains.

A tyre bursts. They wobble on for a few yards. The tyre is flat. They stop.

Another fucking tyre.

Another fucking tyre.

He gets out, jacks up the van. All he has left is a treadless tyre, a tyre naked as a baby, just skin and bone. It will have to do. They

started with three spares, now they have none. He attaches the tyre, unjacks the vehicle.
 They drive.
 It's a long way, she says mildly.
 I know that.
 Well then.
 But we'll get there.

In Istanbul he spent a week writing poems then, halfway to Ankara realised he'd left his poems behind.
 He searches the van from top to bottom.
 I want to go back.
 Why?
 My poems. I left my poems behind.
 So?
 So I want to go back.
 For your poems?
 They were the best I've written.
 Says who?
 Says me, of course. No-one else has read them.
 We can't go back.
 I'm going back.
 I want to go on.
 I want to go back.
 For your poems? They're no good anyway.
 How do you know?
 I know, she says. There are two children in the back of this van, James, in case you hadn't noticed. We're not going back.

They drive on through the ghost roads. Three and half tyres on the van.
 We need to stop. Get some new tyres.
 Yeah right.
 The music starts up again.
 There, can you hear it now?

Dreams and Deceptions

Hear what?
The music.
What music?
The music of
We need to stop.
They stop at a village, change the tyres, drive on.
What about your poems, James?
I lost them. I can't remember them.
What were they about?
You, for fuck's sake. What do you think?
I don't think.

Now the dogs are running towards the highway. Too late he tries to avoid them. One runs straight across the front of the van. He hits the other, at speed, runs straight over it. The dead dog slewed across the road. He doesn't stop.
  Why didn't you stop?
  What, and explain to a bunch of angry Anatolian shepherds armed with guns why I've just killed their dog?
  You should have stopped. Given them something.
  It wasn't my fault. The dog ran straight under the wheels.
  Still, she says, they've lost their dog. They're just shepherds. Those dogs probably cost a fortune.
  They can get another damn dog. I'm not imperilling all of us, you me the children, just because of some dog.

They reach a village, drive down a rutted track looking for accommodation. They've been three days on the road from Istanbul, they need food, shelter, water. They find nothing. Night begins to descend, eyes in the alleys watching them, dogs and children playing on the rutted track.
  There's nothing here, he says. We'd better go on.
  Why go on?
  I thought you wanted to go on.
  You're the one who's always in a hurry.

Anatolia

    I wanted to go back. To find my poems.
    You wouldn't have found them. If you had they wouldn't have been the same.
    What do you mean?
    What do you think I mean?

They drive out of the village, find a place to sleep beneath the stars.
    We're running out of food, she says.
    We'll get some tomorrow.
    Jam tomorrow. And miso.
    There's nothing I can do today.
    I can't wait to get to India.
    I thought I was the one in a hurry.
    You are. I still can't wait to get to India.
    I'm sorry, he says.
    For what?
    I don't know.
    He holds her. She lets him hold her.
    Tomorrow we need to get some food, she says. The children are hungry.

The Devil and Amelia

The pressure on his chest was intense, so intense he could hardly breathe, like an iron ring compressing his chest, an impossible weight; his arms too, by his sides, flattened. He could not lift his arms to save himself. A malignity; the devil come to steal his soul.

Beyond the window, the night was full of stars. The pines barely moved; the loch was lit by starlight. Fish were jumping and a plethora of life filled the hills. Polecats, martins, stoats, foxes, mice, moles, climbing, burrowing, stalking: a rabbit sitting outside its burrow, bathed in starlight. Even the distant thrum of a motor, a ship, some night-prowler. He, inside, fighting for his life.

He thought of all that he had done wrong, as a child and as a man. He could not believe the register. Absolutely everything. He had not done a single thing right.

The pressure on his chest eased for a moment then thumped back down renewed. Greater, more powerful, more terrifying than before. He would cry out but the pressure was everywhere, on his chest, his arms, his throat. He could neither move nor cry out. Then and only then did it begin.

He understood he must destroy this power that overwhelms. Or become just another statistic – I was here and I was not. No longer I, not even a memory.

No-one would miss him. His parents, his sister…a ripple on a river, passed.

He had no children.

He saw his life flash before his eyes – not his past, as books have it, but his future.

The Devil and Amelia

He wakes. Remembers – I had a bad dream. I dreamt the devil was sitting on my chest attempting to pluck out my heart. I had to fight and fight to overcome him. But overcome him I did. I must have believed in something – myself maybe. Though what self that would have been had he failed he has no idea. A constructed self – a self tied together with string. A bundle of selves looming out of the mist like a stranger.

But now I am here.

Sunlight pours through the window and scatters on the loch. An early fishing boat chugs across the horizon. A few early cars on the road.

He rises, washes his face in a basin, pulls on a dressing gown, goes down. She is there, Amelia Honeycutt, the woman he will marry. And yet he barely knows her. How did you sleep? Yes, he says. You slept well? I had a terrible dream. I dreamt the devil was on my chest trying to strangle the life out of me. Strangle? Well, compress. But strangle too. And he had my arms in such a grip I could not move. Poor you, says Amelia.

They carry their breakfast – toast, coffee, muesli, fruit – out onto the veranda that overlooks the loch. A fisherman in waders a hundred yards south. A boat with a sail as far as the eye can see.

Did you dream? he says.

I never dream, says Amelia.

What, never?

Not that I'm aware.

That's strange.

What's strange about it?

Most people dream.

Do they?

I think so.

Well, I don't. I never dream.

She smiles at him and pulls her dressing gown round her legs.

Chilly, even so.

It'll warm up. Just a matter of time.

They gaze out over the loch as they eat their toast.

Dreams and Deceptions

    I thought I was dying.
    Well you weren't.
    I thought I was.
    I'm glad you didn't.
    Me too.
    They sip their coffees. A sudden breeze rattles the eaves of the lodge and the cones of the trees.
    What shall we do today?
    Go down to the loch, wade in. Or maybe a boat ride.
    I'd love a boat ride.
    That's it then.
    Upon the stormy sea.
    It won't be stormy.
    It might.
    But it won't be. He glances up. Look, the sky is blue.
    Birds sing in the trees. Tomorrow he will return to his office and everything will be the same. I nearly died, he thinks. Amelia smiles at him over the rim of her coffee cup. But you didn't. No, but I nearly did. But you even more nearly didn't. One more night. Yes, one more night.

Dr F

Go to the clinic for my appointment with Dr F. He stares at me for a long time then tells me he can see 'terror in my eyes'.

I am slightly drunk. S- is on my mind and I can barely articulate a sentence.

I can't think why I'm here. Dr F is difficult, almost hostile. We agree that I am ambivalent – yes, I am frightened – but of what – the truth?

I am dressed like a cowboy in my boots and leather jacket but I am a fake cowboy.

Dr F sees that I am a fake. He sees 'terror in my eyes'. I tell him everyone has 'terror in their eyes'. He says I can believe that if I want to. He says my barriers are too high, my answers vague and stumbling. He says that I am frightened of revealing my 'dark secrets'. I tell him about S-, how nothing is as it seems. He sees in me a mixture of fear and pride that prevents me being 'accessible'.

I arrived late. I apologised twice, and he asked me why I was apologising. The whole thing was comical to the point of absurdity. He said S- is merely a 'refuge from my problems'. Perhaps sex is a refuge from all problems. I am weak, ill-founded, unsure of myself. My mind is confused. All I want to do is fuck S-.

* * *

Dreams and Deceptions

Last night I shouted at Anne again and S- shouted at me. I shouted at S- to shut up though S- was not my target. S- began to pack a bag. I went next door, sat in a chair, took some aspirin. I returned to bed with earplugs. S- pottered about for a while – going? staying? – then also returned to bed. Why should she leave because of Anne? It makes no sense. I did not shout at or abuse S-. What does it say about S- that S- is prepared to leave simply because I shout at Anne through the ceiling?

It says perhaps our love does not run deep. That our love is no more than a casual fling.

Whereas I am never angry with S-, I was always angry with L-.

*   *   *

Dr F wants to be my friend. But what emerged most of all was leaving. I left, not she. I even once nearly left Dr F. Because, all those years ago, I failed to do so when I had the chance?

Tell him I do not see him as a figure of authority – rather, that I see him as a friend.

Compose a poem, 'The Shocking Apple of my Mother'.

Tell Dr F that I associate sentimentality with self-pity. He says that is a feeling implanted by my father – a rejection of the 'weaker' feelings of love, pity, kindness, compassion.

I fear intimacy. Does Dr F wish to be intimate with me? It is my deepest fear.

I feel guilty. I feel the need to be punished. It is in all of us, perhaps, the need to be punished, to be freed from guilt.

*   *   *

Dr F

S- is gone. The only other person here is me. I hope she returns. But at the same time I realise that may not be what I want.

I said: Our relationship is at a standstill until you tell me the truth. What happened between you? She lost her voice then and spoke all that week in a hoarse whisper. She was desperately sad. She lay on the bed with her face to the wall, listening to the radio. I wasn't cruel or harsh. I didn't shout. But I said, You must tell me. On Saturday she told me. All day she had been unusually attentive to me. She brought me lunch. Later, when I had eaten, she asked if I wanted to go for a walk. I often think, had we gone for that walk, had she told me then, it would have been different. We would have walked and then, by the time we got back, made up.

We were often happy. I was, by and large, kind. I had no wish to hurt her. I was jealous, that was all.

I wanted her happy but I wanted her here. Now she is happy.

I was with D-, she said.

She told me at eight, when I came back from running. She packed her bag while I sat in the bath. By the time I had finished I did not want her to go. But it was too late. We sat in the kitchen and drank tea. We were gentle with each other.

She rose then and held me. I wanted to speak but I didn't. I didn't know what I wanted or what to think. She had never held me like that before. She held me for a long time then let me go. She walked to the door and I followed her. I put my hand on her shoulder and kissed her. I said, I'm very fond of you. Then I watched her leave, her bag over her shoulder, and closed the door.

It was a moment of unbearable pain. I walked inside the flat and howled like a dog. I prayed to God to save me. I wanted nothing except the moment of her return.

*   *   *

Dreams and Deceptions

I am thinking of quitting Dr F. I think he is useless and that the whole thing is useless.

I am frightened, he says. I keep everyone at a distance.
    What am I frightened of? Love, or my craving for love?
    I think the whole idea of 'psychic disorder' is quite insane.
    Am I frightened of who I am?
    He will not see me – 'for various reasons' he says.
    He accuses me of wanting to see the inside of his house.
    He gives me intense looks whenever the subject of buggery comes up.
    I should see Dr G, he says. Dr G will arrange something.

Athens

He is walking barefoot on the road to Athens. A car passes him, stops, reverses back towards him. He has a rucksack on his back and a guitar in his hand. The car stops. A brown eyed girl at the wheel, a blond man with a moustache in the passenger seat.
 Are you going to Athens?
 He checks the car. It is a dusty road stretching for miles in either direction. There isn't much traffic, just them and him.
 He looks at the girl. She looks at him. His eyes are bright blue, almost messianic, his hair brown and curly. His limbs long and slender. He wears an embryonic beard. He doesn't smile.
 Are you going to Athens?
 Yes, he says.
 He climbs into the back of the car. Halfway to Athens she asks if he wants to drive.
 Okay, he says.
 It is months since he's driven a car – back in England before he even set out. The long train journey to the East, the buses, the trains in India, more buses. He doesn't know why he's returning, doesn't even want to return. The fork in the road he took, heading south instead of north, evading the moment of his return. Part of him wants to live on the road for ever. Another part of him longs for home.
 So which is it, she says, staying or going?
 O, staying for now, he says.
 He drives. He realises everything has changed. He is no longer travelling alone. Now he is travelling with this brown-eyed girl, who speaks with an American accent, and her blond boyfriend, David, who doesn't speak at all. They drive past fruit stalls set

Dreams and Deceptions

up by the side of the road selling grapes and melons, tea shacks selling tea in tiny cups, shacks selling bread and flatbread, cheese and wine.
   Soon we'll be in Athens, the girl says.
   Where are you staying?
   We've nothing arranged. We're just heading for the travellers' quarter. Find a cheap hotel.
   And then?
   And then?
   What are your plans?
   O, David wants to go to the islands. Don't you, David?
   We're planning to go to the islands, says David.
   Any particular island?
   No. Any island really. One with sandy beaches and
   Blue skies?
   Yes, says David. Sandy beaches and blue skies.
   Sounds like paradise, he says. He looks at the girl's brown eyes in the rear-view mirror. She is looking back at him.
   And you? she says. Where are you going?
   Nowhere. Nowhere at all. Athens then…more Athens. Maybe the islands.
   Do you want to come with us?
   I don't know.
   They navigate their way through Athens, finally reach the travellers' quarter, a quarter of cheap hotels and bars beneath the Acropolis. The Parthenon looms high on the hill above them.
   Rest up a few days in Athens maybe. I've been travelling for five months.
   You must be tired, says the brown-eyed girl. She introduces herself as Juliette. Like Romeo and Juliet, she says, only with a couple of extra letters at the end.
   In Athens they share a room with three beds. He on one side, David on the other, Juliette in the middle. Next day David wants to go sightseeing. Juliette wants to rest. What are you doing? she says to him. Nothing, he says. Just taking it easy.

David goes sightseeing. They decide to take a walk. Then they take a bus out of town to the temple of Daphni. They sit beneath a fir tree and eat fish and salad and drink wine. They both get slightly drunk. He notices for the first time that Juliette, although a few pounds overweight, has a pretty face. Long dark hair, freckles, full, kissable lips.

Kiss me, says Juliette.

What about David?

We haven't been getting on. I don't want to go to the islands.

He kisses her right there across the table. He reaches under the table for her hand, kisses her again. What now? he says.

They hitchhike back, get a ride on the back of a motorcycle, the two of them squashed together in the pillion seat. He feels his prick stiffening. She feels it too.

What now? I don't know. I've been planning to split up with David anyway.

How long have you been together?

Just over a year. This trip was our big plan. I know what he wants. He wants this to be our courtship, our pre-wedding honeymoon. He wants to get married and have kids. I don't want any of that.

Why not? he says.

Because I don't. Anyway, not with David.

They get back to the hotel. Nothing is said. They sleep three in a row. Next day David goes out again and they spend the afternoon making love in the middle bed. She closes her eyes, curls her knees around his waist and pulls him into her. She is, he thinks, crazy for love. Maybe David didn't love her enough. By the time David gets back from wherever he's been it's obvious though still nothing is said. Next day they are supposed to be going to the islands.

Are we still going to the islands?

I don't know, she says.

I want to go, says David.

You go.

Dreams and Deceptions

Without you?
Yes, she says.
Once again they sleep three in a row. Juliette in the middle. It's only fair to David. Love is tough at the best of times, no need to make it worse. David gets up early. He packs his bag and looks down at her.
Are you sure you won't come?
I'm sure.
Goodbye, he says.
Goodbye, David.

How do you feel?
It's a relief. It would never have worked. I knew it way out, way before we met you.
So I'm just the catalyst.
No.
They spend another week in the hotel, making love and listening to the last Beatles record. The long and winding road. Across the universe. They walk hand in hand up to the Parthenon and back. They return the hire car. They hang out in the hotel with other young travellers smoking dope and listening to music. After a week they hit the road.

Malvern

His mouth aches. At last, he thinks. He has not eaten for two days. He has bought bread and cheese in a shop in the town and climbed into the hills to eat. He brushes back a strand of his long hair caught by the wind. He constructs a cheese roll and digs into it with his teeth.

Last night a man called Scully. Scully was small and sharp-featured, quick-witted, with eyes like little ferrets standing on their hind legs and peering into your soul. Scully embraced him. Now you are here, he said. Scully led him down the hall to a games room and opened a monopoly set. They played monopoly. They played table tennis. He was surprised by Scully's skill at table tennis – quick on his feet, darting into position before the ball could pass him, returning it. He found it difficult to get the better of Scully despite his good eye. In the end he vanquished Scully. Sit by me, he said, and they sat, with tea. Now, said Scully, tell me more about yourself. Do you have a girlfriend? I do not, he said.

The sun struck like lightning through holes in the sky through which poured ladders of light and, descending the ladders, angels. Beams of light, as though God were shining a torch through holes in the sky. Peering down at him. He expected at any moment to hear a voice from the clouds: This is my beloved Son, in whom I am well pleased. A strange remark really. Only five more miles, he thinks. He will walk. Another five miles past empty corn fields and trees abutting the roadside and the light shining down through holes in the sky and the grave voice uttering. This is my beloved Son. In whom I am well pleased.

Dreams and Deceptions

It was a lie of course. 'I have no girlfriend,' he said – except it was not really a lie. He had, would have, such a companion. In the moment of which we speak he did not. No, he said, I don't. He sipped his tea. It was the first tea he had drunk, the first drink of any sort other than water, since the day he had set out. He had set out, walking to the end of the long drive that led to his parents' house, and hitchhiked west, short lifts for the most part, towards Malvern. What I will do there is find myself: that and jot down a few poems in the notebook he always carried. The notebook was lemon-green. The pencil was blue. He jotted down poems and each poem gave him renewed energy as though by writing the poem he had re-created himself. Have I re-created myself. What do I wish to be or, more to the point, not be. What have I come here to get away from. *This is my beloved Son, in whom I am well pleased.*

Destruction, he thinks, is at the heart of creation. The first, or possibly second, law of thermodynamics. Yet are laws laws? They are not immutable. They can change. It is a matter of perception. What we believe is what we see not vice versa. We observe it to be true and thereby contort ourselves to make it true. Nothing is created and nothing destroyed. Yet everything is and falls like fat from a pan through holes in the sky or the cumulus that surrounds us. Drip fed like nectar to the gods below.

More tea? enquired Scully. Scully had long girlish fingers and wore a green coat. He was slim and slight with ferret features and darting brown eyes. He would at some point make a pass at him. It would be pointless, he wasn't of that persuasion. Still he felt a degree of ease in the company of Scully. Scully was talking, twisting and turning meaning sideways and backwards, contorting it till it revealed itself in some way or other that suited him. Scully the realist was not a realist of the possible. Who is. Possibility is that which lies beyond our reach that we cannot control. Possibility is itself and is not beholden to our will though we may think it so. Possibility is that which is already written that we do not know.

His mouth aches. He cannot take another bite. The sun is implacable. He lies on the stringy grass, flies buzz round his face and alight on his lips and eyelids. I am not dead, he thinks, not quite. He has another thought: I will not, cannot die. He feels himself to be immortal. In a sense he is. The likelihood of his dying in the near future is small. Disappearing like the white rabbit into a hole of varying size. I will not die whatever I do nor fail to die. I will sleep or not sleep but if I sleep I will wake. I cannot die. Even when I die I will not be dead. I will merely be awake elsewhere.

Scully's hand, now, rather forwardly, upon his knee. He is too relaxed, too inert, to remove it. He feels drowsy, so drowsy he thinks he will sleep. Scully is telling him of other things. About the time he was mistaken for a thief in Tangier. I was incarcerated for three weeks with hardened criminals and hardly the space to lie upon the hard floor, Scully is saying. His hand moves upwards along his thigh. With an effort of will which he cannot analyse and barely effect he pushes Scully's hand back down and moves his leg away. Scully's hand returns though this time remains stationary. Scully continues talking. I saw a man whipped till the blood ran, he is saying.

His mouth aches. One bite was all it took. The bite he has been anticipating for two days: sinking his teeth into the soft mush of the bread, tasting the tang of the cheese, and all at once the pain. Devouring through his tears until the pain becomes too great and he stops. He stops altogether. He does not understand: Why, he asks, does my mouth ache? Scully is sitting by his bedside stroking his arm. Now his leg again. Scully's fingers seem magnetically drawn to his leg. He is past caring. He asks Scully to fetch him a cigarette. Scully unperturbed does as he is bidden. Well goodnight, he says. In the morning he is gone.

Halfway down the steep hill, halfway down the shingle track that leads towards the harbour and the sea, a man comes chasing after him. The man smiles at him as though he is an imbecile. Have you swept? he says. Have I swept? I do not believe you have swept. The man mistakes him for an imbecile. Back up the single track he goes, with the man, to sweep. He sweeps and the man releases him from his indenture.

He goes to the road, sits down and waits. He will play a game with stones. His game absorbs him to the point where he forgets about procuring a lift and thinks only of his game with the stones. He splits himself like an amoeba into various participants in this game of stones. One he calls Lattrick, another Finoyne, another, for want of any other, Scully. Scully he imagines as a small dark man with sharp features and quick brown eyes. What if Scully and I were the only ones left? We would no doubt kill each other. Or, rather, one would kill the other, unless they killed each other at the same moment. That is unlikely. He thinks of the story of two brothers who died simultaneously: which one's child or children would inherit the kingdom?

A fly finds its way into his mouth: he is too tired, too inert to move. All these years, he thinks, and what have I to show for them? To show whom? says a second voice. Whomever I am trying to impress, he says. Why are you trying to impress anyone? says the second voice. I don't know, he says. Is life worth living? In your case perhaps not, says the second voice.

Voices, voices. Am I alone. I am alone. There is, upon this hillside, only I. He sits up, takes another bite of his cheese roll, lies back down. He chews slowly, painfully, the masticated mush sticking to the raw roof of his mouth. It is too painful to eat: perhaps that is it. Too painful to eat, too painful to live: that is why we die, though which comes first the chicken or the egg. Which goes first, the younger or the elder. Whose children inherit the kingdom. What kingdom.

Night will fall. He knows it to be true, knows that he cannot arrest the passage of time, but pays no attention. I must move, he thinks. A second voice cajoles: Why move? What is there to move for? Why move from a to b when they are both in the end the same? From a to b and back again. That is all. Avoiding or evading difficulty and unpleasantness as best one can only falling deeper into difficulty and unpleasantness with every move. One may as well not move and yet one moves.

What, he wonders, had I allowed Scully to have his way. Would it have been so bad? He wonders what Scully would have done. Reached for his cock and balls, he presumes, to stroke or fondle them as the man had when he was a boy. Kissed him perhaps. No, not kissed him; fondled and squeezed more likely. All the while talking. Was he a man or a woman? He imagines Scully as a woman, a small brown-eyed brunette with sharp not soulful features. Too knowing, too demanding. He would not have desired Scully as a partner in sex. He was not gay. Scully perhaps too. How many gay men are really gay?

Now he feels sorry, not for himself but for Scully. Lurking like a spider in his wayside hostel, weighing up each newcomer that they might succumb or be turned or do they already face the same way? A lonely life. Yet it need not be. Perhaps one day Scully too will find his soulmate as some it is said do. A living death. Does he have a girlfriend. He has a girl. She is in London. She too is perhaps waiting.

His mouth aches and yet he wants, more than anything, another bite. The hunger, he thinks, and the passion. The passion and the hunger. Of our lives. Our lives, what are they. A life. His life. An ant's or a fly's. Unknowing yet what do we know. The ant or the fly perhaps. What do they see that we don't see. The ant, the fly. A different world. Not the world that we see. The fly, the ant. The fly flies, it is a life of the air. The ant crawls. No, not crawls. Scuddles. Rapidly upon several long legs. Six, at a guess. Scuddles upon six legs and we are vast beyond imagining. The ant cannot imagine us. A size so enormous it is impractical even to contemplate. Natural objects as mountains and rivers are natural objects. The ant does not see mountains and rivers, merely enormity. Objectless, empty space. The sky is blue dotted with white clouds. Layers of cream, strands of white, weightless, unencumbered. Only space immeasurable. Only trunkless legs of

Dreams and Deceptions

stone. What does an ant or a fly know? The fly perhaps as it flies upwards and conquers space. The ant conquers eternity as the fly conquers space.

He lies upon the grass upon the hill. His bag of books beside him. Today he will meet Scully. Last night in a hostel in a town. There was no-one there. He waited for an eternity, no-one came. He rapped upon the counter. He remained quite still. This absence. This presence. He went, or might have gone, to a drinks dispenser the size of a small mountain. The drinks dispenser dispensed nothing. Still he waited. Upon another night, upon a French beach, beside a mountain, beneath a castle. He and his girlfriend. Does he have girlfriend? Scully will ask. He does not. He does. And yet she, if she exists, is not present. Perhaps she does not exist. Perhaps, despite the stillness and the silence, the place is alive and he alone is not.

A trip with lbc

The Frenchman stopped and stared. He was naked apart from a pair of dirty Y-fronts and looked as if he hadn't shaved for two days.

Charles, said lbc.

I smiled and began to hold out my hand but thought better of it.

He will stay the night, said lbc. I hope that's alright.

U-huh, said Charles.

I deduced he'd been sleeping – it was, after all, after midnight. The streets below were still alive with the sound of people celebrating. Up here, at the top of the building, the sounds were muffled. Still loud, but not loud enough to keep the Frenchman awake.

The Frenchman went away. lbc showed me my room. The room was sparsely furnished, with a blind that didn't keep out the light and an ancient chest of drawers. I made up the bed, he said, waving his hand towards it. I pulled back the covers; the sheets looked clean enough. lbc went to the kitchen to fetch tumblers and we sat on the only two chairs in the sitting room, beneath a vast painting of a naked woman surrounded by elephants and leopards, and drank wine. I pulled a reefer from the inside pocket of my leather jacket. We smoked it in silence.

I haven't smoked for years, said lbc.

It's not very strong, I said. But it was and we sat there with our heads spinning.

When are you leaving?

Tomorrow.

Dreams and Deceptions

Going back south?
I shrugged. I would go back eventually – to the ones who missed me. Though why they missed me I didn't know.
lbc rubbed his eyes and smiled.
I've been on the road for five days.
I waved the reefer in the air.
This is quite strong.
I haven't smoked a reefer for twenty years.
What do you do?
I'm writing a book.
What about?
The Scots.
What Scots?
The Scots who went to America. Did you know that half the population of Scotland went to America?
My ancestors were Scots who went to America, I said. Then I said, I need to go to Slaters. To buy a jacket.
I'm suing English Heritage, said lbc, handing me the reefer. They've no idea.

I tiptoed to the bathroom in the night so as not to awake the Frenchman. I didn't want to see the Frenchman again. I pushed a chair up against the door. On my third excursion I forgot about the chair, hit it hard with my right ankle and went down yelping. I was aware of the absurdity of the situation – rolling around on the bare floor of an almost empty flat in the middle of the night clutching my ankle and yelping – and began to laugh. I was laughing so hard there were tears rolling down my cheeks.
Fuck, I said out loud. Fuck!
I heard sounds of movement from the next door room and went quiet, clutching my ankle, trying neither to yelp nor laugh. I heard the Frenchman cross the room, pause, then quietly open the door. I'd no idea which way he was heading. The chair had flipped over on its side when I crashed into it so I had little protection.
I said to lbc,

A trip with lbc

Is the Frenchman safe?

I can't vouch for him, said lbc. He's a philosopher. Push something up against the door perhaps.

Now I held my breath and clutched my ankle as the Frenchman exited his room. He walked past my door and headed for the bathroom. I heard the toilet flush. I heard the door open and the Frenchman exit. Then suddenly I couldn't hear him any more.

Fuck, I said under my breath.

An image of Raskolnikov flashed into my mind. The perfect crime. Who knew I was there, bar lbc and the Frenchman?

He was waiting. Not breathing. Just standing and waiting. Waiting, I guessed, for me to make a move.

I felt myself falling, like a Russian soldier, into the deep. Don't sleep, I urged myself. Aware once again of the absurdity of the situation I stifled a laugh. Maybe the Frenchman heard me, maybe not. He began to move. I heard him move past my door towards his room. Heard his door open and shut. Then it was daylight and the sounds of the street starting up.

The rain fluttered lightly against the window like the wings of dead souls or the revellers from the night before. The planet is crammed full of life as though all the life in the universe were there though the universe is no more than a figment of our imagination. The wastes of space no more than a two-dimensional hinterland between the world of the living and the world of the dead.

Some see and hear both.

The Frenchman was asleep. I put my ear to his door and could hear the sound of rhythmic breathing. I imagined him sprawled on the otherwise empty bed with the sheet tangled between his filthy legs. I performed some stretching exercises in the sitting room beneath the painting of the naked girl facing down the elephants and leopards (or rising above them). Four storeys below stragglers from the night met office workers on their way to work. A dustcart slowly swept the street, hissing and crying like an abandoned child.

Dreams and Deceptions

I found a packet of cereal in the kitchen and poured some of its contents into a bowl. There was nothing to moisten it with but water. I took the concoction back to the living room and sat at the only table with my back to the window while I ate. I'd be finished and gone before the Frenchman rose. What his purpose was, I had no idea. I had a wife and child in the south and needed to be home soon.

I walked to the door and put down my bag then went back to check the bedroom and kitchen for anything I might have left behind. There was nothing but still I had strange reluctance to leave, to cast myself as it were like a leaf upon the waters. I stood in the passage beneath a large silver-framed print of a railroad with wires and posts in the shape of crosses receding into the bleak distance. I took a deep breath and opened the door.

A woman in her thirties with a pale complexion and long ginger hair came out of the flat on the other side of the landing.

Who are you?

I stayed the night.

Here?

Yes. I'm a friend of lbc.

That's as may be, she said. But I've never heard of lbc.

This is his flat.

Is it? she said.

She passed by me and I watched as she descended the steep spiralling stairs towards the street until the sound of her footsteps and the sight of her long ginger hair were gone. I wondered whether our conversation had really happened or whether I had made it up. I followed her down to the street. The sound of the meandering dustcart was deafening as the machine sluiced slowly through pools of rainwater on its way to some far-off depot.

Rosa

The record was going round and round, said Cass. Round and round. *The first cut is the deepest.* Round and round all night long it went. Eventually I broke the door down and...

Broke the door down bollocks, said Rosa. She didn't break the door down. She knocked on the door and came in. The door wasn't even locked.

It was. And she was lying on her bed with her wrists slashed. 'O Rosa,' I said.

Fuck off, said Rosa.

Well, yeah, that's what you did say. Or wanted to say. You certainly gave me a 'fuck off' look. You didn't realize you were dying.

I knew perfectly well I was dying. I'd drunk a bottle of vodka.

You knew you were drunk. You didn't know you were dying.

You don't know what I knew.

Yes I do. You said 'I'm dying. Fuck off.'

I thought you said she didn't say anything, I said. I thought she just gave you a 'fuck off' look.

Cass looked at me pityingly.

She said 'I'm dying fuck off'. Is that so strange? She was in love with this girl you see. The one she travelled a hundred miles through the night for and...

That girl was you, said Rosa. Isn't that right, Cassie?

Help me make up a bed, said Cass.

No, I said.

Rosa was sitting at my feet, her head resting against my knee,

Dreams and Deceptions

snoring. From time to time she gave a little start, like a dog in a basket startled by dreams of the chase.

You're not sleeping with her, you know, said Cass.

She went next door to make up the bed.

There's no point, I said. I'm not sleeping in it. I'd rather sleep on the floor.

Well you can't. You'll sleep here. She tossed a double sheet over to me. I caught it and for a moment the sheet billowed between us like a sail in the wind.

Cass laughed.

There, she said. It's an adventure. Did your mummy tuck you up when you were small?

I suppose so. Didn't yours?

Mine did. Rosa's didn't. Rosa's mummy was always too drunk.

She raised her voice, turning her head towards the open door. Wasn't she, Rosa?

We walked by the lake. Rosa crouched down and looked at her reflection in the water.

She puckered her lips.

I'm beautiful, she said.

She turned to look at me.

Would you rather go to bed with a beautiful man or an ugly woman?

I don't know. A beautiful man probably.

Who?

Tell me about you and Cass.

Why?

I'd like to know.

Who?

Rosa you're impossible.

No I'm not. She stood up, put her arm in mine, pressed herself to me. Looked up at me with her heart-mouth and her opaque eyes. I'm possible. *Everything*'s possible. Don't you know that?

O Rosa.
Don't 'O Rosa' me.
Everything's not possible. To you maybe. Not to anyone else.
Why's that then?
You tell me.
Because you want to fuck me and you're scared.
I'm not scared.
Rosa laughed.
Yes you are. Cass told me.
Where were you last night then? I said, changing the subject.
Not sleeping with you, to be sure. Do you like music? She led me up the hill and along an avenue of trees to Kenwood House where a string quartet was playing. She wrinkled her pretty nose.
This isn't the sort of music I like. What sort of music do you like?
I don't know. Dylan...
Dylan, she said. Dylan. Don't give me Dylan. It's depressive music. Don't you like happy music? I like happy music. Music you can sing along to. You can't sing along to Dylan.
You can. To some of it.
Bollocks you can. It's all groaning and whining. I like music with a bit of life to it.
How long have you known Cass?
Too long. Come on. Let's go and look at the swans. I love swans. They're so beautiful and fierce.

She sat on the floor swaying slightly from side to side and moaning.
O Rosa, said Cass.
She's drunk.
I can see that.
I went out to make some tea. I sat in the kitchen smoking a cigarette while I watched the kettle boil. I was trying to decide whether to stay or go. On the one hand I was falling in love with

Dreams and Deceptions

Rosa. On the other, Anitra Shore was having an opening that night at her dance studio and I thought there might be someone there – someone easier, someone new, maybe even Anitra Shore herself.

Manesh

One day, clip-clopping around his hut in his wooden shoes, Manesh stopped suddenly and pointed to something just above my head.

Guava!

I looked up. I could see nothing. I looked closer. There, in the guava tree, just above my head, hung a single guava.

It is a sign to mark your coming! Never before has that tree borne any fruit. Before you came, that tree was barren!

He reached up, plucked the fruit, handed it to me with a smile. He was like a warrior with his dark eyes and his black beard.

Do you like guavas? Let us go inside.

He clip-clopped into his tiny hut, which had just room enough for the two of us. At night we slept on either side of the open fire. The hut had a hole in the roof for a chimney; when the rains came, it flooded.

We sat on our respective sides of the fire and shared the guava.

It is a miracle; I have been here three years and there has never been a guava on that tree. How could it have grown unnoticed? It means that someone special has come.

He lifted my flute to his lips and blew. He had his own, highly original, style of playing: puffing out the notes and sliding his finger over the holes, creating half-notes and unexpected discords.

We shall have a feast! A feast to celebrate your coming! We will invite everyone! But it will cost money. Do you have money?

How much?

He smiled easily.

O, not very much. Say, a hundred rupees?

Okay. It wasn't much – a lot less than the merchant from Ladakh had stolen from me.

Good. We will only need to buy food – everything else is free. He went back to his flute playing then handed it to me.

Play something, he said, and lay back on his pillow, his hands folded behind his head, his eyes closed, a slight smile upon his lips. I played a piece my sister had taught me. It had been her flute once. Take good care of it, she said, when she gave it to me; this is precious to me. Now, it belonged to Manesh.

Food was bought. Servants appeared from nowhere. Manesh went around the boundaries of his territory, puffing out his cheeks and blowing his conch shell over and over, blowing, walking a few paces, blowing again. Gurus appeared all over the hillside, some hopping, some walking, some being led. Manesh blew and gurus came until at last twelve had assembled. Of disparate appearance and demeanour: some old, some young, some quiet, some garrulous, some tall, some short, some handsome, some plain. The oldest was a man of grave visage and a long grey beard, led by a much younger man; the noisiest a young man with cross eyes who shouted, laughed and gesticulated crossly and could not, it seemed, keep quiet.

I chopped wood with the servants: one foot on the log, the axe in my hand. I was used to chopping wood but compared to them my chopping was clumsy. A wiry servant, half my size, took the axe from my hand with a gleaming smile, put one bare foot on each log to hold it steady and sliced through it with a single blow.

When the pile was finished, still smiling, he handed the axe back to me.

The noisy guru shouted and gesticulated. I could not understand what about. The old man sat gravely at the table, listening but not looking. I realised he was blind.

The table was situated on a bank above the hut. The servants prepared the food and gathered leaves to serve as plates. The gurus took their places at the table. Then Manesh, who had been occupied greeting his fellow-gurus, remembered me. Where was I to sit? For a moment he was nonplussed. I couldn't sit at the table with the gurus because I wasn't a guru, nor even a Brahmin; but nor could I sit with the servants, who were sitting in a huddle on the grass beside the hut. He came to a decision. He pointed to a smaller bank just below and to the side of the bank where the table was set.

You will sit there, he said, smiling. That will be your place.

Manesh the handsome, Manesh the impresario, sat in the middle, the sun shining on his handsome, aquiline face, his long black hair resting on his shoulders. He was flanked by his fellow-gurus, six on either side. The sun was high; the hills, bare on the lower levels until they reached their tree-clad summits, sheared upwards towards a cloudless sky. Below, the river wound slowly through the valley, sparkling in the sunlight.

The noisy ones shouted, the grave ones were grave, the silent ones were silent. Manesh sat in the midst, smiling and at ease, like a latter-day Christ. The servants brought food to the table then threw it from a short distance onto the leaves. Then it was my turn; sitting cross-legged and awkward on my bank, the food thrown onto my leaf from a short distance. As though I too were a Brahmin; as though I too were an honoured guest.

When the feast was eaten and cleared away, and the gurus vanished back into the hills, Manesh and I sat together in his tiny hut beside an open fire. It was time for me to leave. I had been given the name of a sitar teacher in Benares, a player who had once taught Ravi Shankar. Though Manesh was more worldly-wise than Guru Maharaji, had been to university and spoke perfect English, there was nothing more I could learn from him.

We slept in the smoky hut on either side of the dying embers. In the morning, as always, he was up before me, clip-clopping in his

Dreams and Deceptions

wooden sandals round the tiny hut. There was a small guava tree beside the hut; he looked up and espied a single guava.

This a miracle, he said, for the tree is barren.

Before I left I handed him the flute. He took it without a word.

Look after it, I said. Or pass it on.

I gathered my few belongings and walked down the hillside towards the Chenab River.

The Gardens

They sit on a blanket with the picnic set out on the grass beside them. They are joined by his mother's friend, Jeanette, and her two sons, Edward and James. Edward and James are older than he is. He does not know them. James is three years older, svelte and sleek, with black curly hair and blue eyes. Edward, who does not resemble his brother, is one year older. James and Edward climb a tree while he watches. James sits beside Jeanette. Jeanette ruffles James's hair.

Cosmo fell off a swing and cracked his head open, says Jeanette.

O, says his mother. That's unfortunate.

Yes, says Jeanette. Cracked his head right open as though a spade had sliced it through. Bits of ear and brain spilling out. Lots of blood.

Was nobody there? says his mother.

Nobody where, dear? says Jeanette.

Yes, says his mother. She picks up a plate of cucumber sandwiches and hands them to Jeanette. Jeanette takes one, pops it into her mouth and starts chewing.

Yes, blood everywhere. You can still see the stains.

Did nobody come?

The park-keeper came. You know, that fat bloke with the great bunch of keys attached to his waist like ha ha ha. She lifts her hand to cover her mouth. Like like

What did he do? says his mother.

Dropped down dead, says Jeanette.

Dead? says his mother.

129

Dreams and Deceptions

Well not quite dead. But down. As though he too had been sliced open with a spade.

Sandwich? says his mother. She holds out the plate to him. He takes one.

So there they were, says Jeanette. In a heap. The pair of them. You couldn't help laughing.

Why? says his mother.

Why what? says Jeanette.

Why did he drop down dead?

Fainted, says Jeanette. Keeled over like a whale. With his keys O ha ha ha. Ha. A crumbly mash of bread and cucumber appears on her lips. It really was too funny for words. The two of them. In a heap. Cosmo – poor Cosmo – and that fat man. Spaced out like tailor's dummies. Cosmo with his head split open, oozing blood, and that great fat man lying there with his keys.

Did no-one help? says his mother.

No-one was able to, says Jeanette. Here. She rifles through her bag. I have some Dairylea. Does your boy liked Dairylea?

No, says his mother. I don't think so.

Ah well, says Jeanette.

Would you like to climb a tree? asks Edward.

He climbs a tree with Edward. James remains with his mother eating sandwiches. His mother ruffles his hair. The sound of their voices fades as they climb though he can still hear them – Jeanette speaking in exclamations, his mother's cool interventions. James says nothing, just lies with his head on his mother's lap while she feeds him cheese. They reach the top.

Don't fall off, says Edward.

Did that boy really get his head split open?

Yes, I think so. I didn't see it.

Where were you?

At home.

Where was your mother?

At home.

The Gardens

So she didn't see it either?

No. At least I don't think so. He takes a gingerbread man out of his pocket and hands it to him. He eats it, feeling the thick succulent sugar on his tongue. There are birds flying in the sky. From the top of the tree they can see large white houses beyond the gardens and the tops of buses in the road. The sounds fade into silence.

Do you like Dairylea?

Yes, says Edward. Race you down.

They climb down, hand over hand. Edward reaches the ground first. Their mothers are still talking about the accident.

Well, yes, in the end. But it was a sight, says Jeanette. The two of them there in a heap. They took longer to revive the park keeper than Cosmo. Apparently he hit his head on the way down. Don't know how you'd tell the difference if you ask me. Another sandwich? He was the only one with a key. They had to go through all the keys till they found the key that unlocked the gate. Eventually they found it. The ambulance meandered through. Two men in uniforms put him on a stretcher and carried him away. They tended to his head first. He'll never be the same. The park keeper was too fat to lift. They gave him smelling salts and slapped his face. He opened his eyes. Where am I? he said.

What did they say?

What did who say?

The ambulance men?

In the park, they said. On the ground. You have fallen. Did I fall? he said.

He sat up and wiped his nose with the back of his hand. He too had blood pouring out of his head. Another sandwich? James looks up at the sky and wriggles with pleasure. I must have fallen, he said. They patched him up. They didn't take him away. They patched him up and he sat there with a bandage on his head while they drove away with Cosmo.

Dreams and Deceptions

Do you have any daughters?

Yes, one. Samantha. I don't know why I say that. It isn't true. Do you?

No, says his mother.

After their picnic they go to the playground to play on the swings. Don't fall off! Jeanette says. No, I mean, it's a once in a lifetime thing, isn't it? Falling off I mean. How do you fall off, anyway? If you hang on you don't fall off.

Perhaps he didn't hang on.

Can't have done. Or maybe he went right over the top. We'll never know. Poor Cosmo. His poor mother.

James stays close to his mother while he plays with Edward. They play on the swings and the slide and in the sandpit. James does some jumps in the sandpit then returns to his mother.

Home.

Home?

Yes, boys, home. The boys stand dutifully, almost at attention, beside her.

The Runner

He stood in the small passageway jogging slowly up and down on the spot then threw himself to the floor and performed ten quick press-ups. He pressed his hands against the doorframe and rose on his toes to his full height before subsiding onto his heels; breathing in, holding his breath, repeating the manoeuvre twenty times as Warner had said. He laced up his shoes and tied a red bandanna round his head.

He jogged through the town, increasing his pace as he ran beside the castle, then slowed to a walk. The town was full of holiday-makers but few looked at or even noticed him. Two overweight women stood outside the ironmongers blocking his path but he stepped into the road and jogged round them. He stopped, checked his watch and put one foot on the bench outside the Black Swan to tighten a shoelace.

He breathed deeply and swung his arms twice around his head, checked his watch again, crouched like a sprinter, clicked his watch to 'start' and set off. Ran down the slope past the entrance to the cattle market and up alongside the church where, years before, he had married a woman and where, a year later, his daughter had been baptised. Standing in the porch with the child in his arms as cameras whirred and clicked, as they embraced friends and strangers and then walked back together through the town towards her grandmother's house where she, dead now, had sat unmoving in the middle of the garden wearing a red hat while the sun's rays beat down upon it.

He stepped into the road to pass two children and continued past parked cars in the direction of the river. He had done this run many times and knew precisely the distances; a quarter mile to the small housing estate, round a bend where he once more assumed the pavement, through an even smaller estate of more expensive houses where the priest and his friend Michael the Steward lived, half a mile to the trellis wall where half-wild roses grew, past the pill factory and back onto the main road towards the town, past roadside cottages, a bus-stop and a fire station to the Black Swan. One mile exactly. Nothing ever changed. Every day, every run, the same.

From the Black Swan he ran down the hill towards the bridge. He checked his watch to discover that he was running a few seconds faster than usual and reduced his pace for otherwise, he knew, he would struggle up the long hill beside the farm, perhaps even slow to a walk as he did more and more often these days. On the trail through the wood, muddier than usual, he slowed to avoid slipping, maybe falling, maybe tumbling through the trees and into the river far below. He thought once again of his wife, though he had not seen her for two years and did not know where she was, only that her occasional emails were not friendly and that money still went monthly from his account to hers without acknowledgement. He began to see, as the rain eased off and a bleak sun slivered through the thin branches of the trees, that his only crime was being weak – too weak to have resisted her then, too weak to resist her now.

He nearly slipped and fell beside the wooden fence that had been erected at the spot where another runner had slid and tumbled through the thin trees, bouncing and clawing and ending up in the river far below with his head bashed in, whose life had only been saved by the presence of a fisherman standing in the middle of the river with green waders up to his hips who had mistaken him for a fish. His hand reached out to balance against the fence

The Runner

and steer him back onto the path which rose and fell through the wood, past and over the exposed roots of trees, down a slope to where a tree had fallen, down a steeper slope to the first gate. He barely broke his stride as he flicked the catch, pushed open the gate and ran leaving the gate to swing shut behind him. Across the field beside the river where yet another tree, an ancient oak, had fallen, where most days he saw a buzzard and where once he had seen a family camping, a man, a woman and a very fat young girl.

He saw them crossing the bridge and stopping beside a Ducato camper van and had engaged the man in conversation. Was it a good van? Was it fast? Was it comfortable, economical? He had thought then of nothing but escape. Now they were camping and he did not acknowledge them for he did not recognise them, so full was his head with memories and plans for the future.

To his right the river, less restless here, as though knowing the worst (the falling, the tumbling, the shattering, through mountains and mountain villages, carrying whatever fate decreed within its flow) were over; where once families of swans nested and paddled unhurried through the rushes. Towards the end of the field, before another spinney of trees, there was a dip, often waterlogged, which he skirted, leaping the worst of it. Up a short muddy slope to a spinney of trees and through the trees to a second field, taking the higher and drier of two sheep-tracks, alongside a copse of trees to a second gate, a gate alongside a hedge where he had once watched a family of redstarts fluttering down to seize their prey before fluttering back up to devour it.

It was years since he had seen a redstart, years since the river had been calm enough for swans to nest. Years since he had been able to run as he once had, swift as the wind; years since his daughter had been born. The years had slipped past without him noticing, except that the view in the mirror changed year by year,

135

Dreams and Deceptions

the face that had once been young was now old. He observed the requirements of time without ever quite believing in them but without the strength to deny or refute them, without the strength to disappear. 'I trail myself around with me wherever I go' a prisoner had written once as he abandoned his bid for freedom. 'Life is a cruel joke' someone else wrote though it didn't seem much like a joke to him, not anyway for those whose lives were taken from them. 'Everyone dies, in the end, from a wish to die' though a wish to die was nothing more than a wish for oblivion. 'We procreate and then regret it' someone else had said though perhaps we regret it more if we don't.

The field was full of sheep, mothers with lambs, though the lambs were bigger and sturdier now, bigger and sturdier than they had been even a few days ago and they stood their ground and watched him with a mixture of indifference and hostility as he ran towards them. The sheep would scatter, the lambs running back to their mothers, their mothers moving a safe distance away, as he ran across the middle of the field towards the next gate, a gate that led to a twenty-acre arable field that led in turn to the long incline up beside the farm where so often these days he was forced to slow to a walk. Two lambs in particular, male lambs almost the size of their mothers, stared at him as he ran towards them but didn't budge. He was puzzled by this, running straight towards them, as though somehow they had lost their fear of him. As he approached, instead of running away the lambs bucked and moved towards him, their bright green eyes trained upon him like laser beams, like lambs from another world. But we all come from another world, he thought. He was almost upon them now and still they hadn't turned, just bucked and moved towards him. Others too were moving towards him. He tried to run round the two male lambs but as did so the one nearest him lowered its head and charged, bashing him on the leg, throwing him sideways. He slipped and fell, then quickly rose as the other sheep, emboldened by the performance of the lambs, encircled him.

He turned to run back but the sheep behind were also moving towards him, their guttural bleating cries now filled with menace. They were quicker than he was. A stout ewe blocked his path and he tripped and fell headlong. They came in with their heads, their teeth, their hooves, all the fear drained out of them, his pitiful cries as nothing in the still, warm air.

The Gallery

The blind girl worked in a bar and could pull the drinks and locate the customers and take the money and deliver the change. One day someone left open the trapdoor to the cellar and she fell into the hole and damaged her head on the steps and passed out. After that she sold ice-creams through a hatch at the side of the bar to passers-by. Then she met and married the owner of Pendragon Court. He was a young man with prominent Adam's apple and lank hair that flopped over the side of his head. As they came in, she took his arm. She had a dog, but she left the dog outside.

She conversed with my son, looking straight at him.
    Who are you?
    My son told her.
    What do you do?
    He told her that too – he was an artist.
    I love art, she said. I love paintings. Do you paint?
    He explained – sometimes he used paint, sometimes chalk and crayon.
    Do you paint portraits? she asked.
    My son didn't know she was blind.
    Yes, would you like to see them?
    Yes, very much.
    He went upstairs and came down with his portfolio. He opened the portfolio and laid out the drawings on a table-top. She bent forward to study them with him. She ran her fingertips across the faces of the drawings. She asked him,
    Who is this one of?
    Me.

The Gallery

I thought so. You see a great deal, don't you?
My son explained. He went to art class every Tuesday...he drew...his teacher supervised and helped him.
But you don't need any help, do you? said the blind girl. You already understand what you see?
He had had a troubled life. Abandoned by his parents as a child, brought up by his grandparents...now, years later, he was getting to know his father for the first time, helping him in his gallery.
But you know what you see, don't you? persisted the blind girl, her hands on the drawing, her eyes fixed on him.
I draw what my art teacher wants me to draw, he said.
I love to draw too, said the blind girl. Trouble is, my drawings go all over the place...I lose track of the lines on the paper. But I know what I see. But you...you draw exactly what you see.

Her name was Isabel. She walked through the town with her dog and sometimes with the young landowner she had married. He was an expert at restoring old cars; she, by contrast, was an artist. Her life was devoted to art, to the visions she saw in her head.
She said to me,
I can't draw for toffee. I so envy those who can. Don't you?
Of course. I used to love drawing. My son is very good.
I know, I was talking to him. I loved his work. It was so...intense.
He is intense. Probably too intense.
O no, she said. It is better to be intense. Life is short. You don't get second chances. What do you do, apart from running the gallery?
Well...I watch birds.
O yes? And what's you favourite?
I like raptors best...eagles, buzzards. Kites. And kestrels – I love kestrels. There is no other bird so pretty and so fierce.
I see. Is that why they call you 'Billy Kestrel'?
How did you know that?

Dreams and Deceptions

O, I see things other people don't. That's the advantage of being blind. You see things other people don't.
Like an artist.
We are all artists, she said, but not all of us know it.

Michael and his shaven-headed acolyte came out of the night. The acolyte, whose name was Stephen, put his arms around the poet, John Child, and they fell into a tight embrace. They had been friends since their time on the East River, long before the days when he too became a purveyor of art, before he became a follower of Michael.

I have little appreciation of the visual arts, Michael said.
We can't all be good at everything. It doesn't matter. Art is what means something. Or what something means. If it doesn't mean anything it isn't art.
Must art have a meaning?
Of course – though artists like to deny it. But they are not reliable. Artists are like junkies – there is always something they love more...
Michael shivered.
Junkies, he said. What a terrible word. A life devoted literally to rubbish, to junk. Never once lifting your eyes to the stars...
Even so, it is a life of devotion. A sort of devotion.
But not a selfless devotion...not a sacrifice of self for a higher good.
A sacrifice of self...but no, not for a higher good. Or god. A lesser god...the devil, perhaps.
O, we don't believe in that sort of thing these days, said Michael.
He turned to one of the paintings.
It seems very...childlike.
It is very childlike. But look at this... I pointed out one of John Child's earlier paintings on a neighbouring wall: complex, at once symbolic and representational. Two naked girls dancing around

a gallows in an Arizona-like desertscape with a river running through and a ship on the river.

So much in one painting.

Past, present and future symbolised by the river. Do you see, right in the corner, where the river forks?

And yet death-obsessed. Quite obsessed with death.

Many mediaeval paintings depicted death in some way or other. With a flattened skull...

But life is not about death, said Michael. Death is the other side, the other face of the coin....like the dark side of the moon. We cannot escape from it, and one day it will embrace us...but death is no more than the end of life. While we live we must live ...face death down.

He is facing death down...look at the women. They are dancing, despite it all.

Yes, said Michael. I am beginning to see them in a different light.

My Father's House

I am wearing a wide-brimmed hat as I walk down the winding drive in the summer sun towards my father's house. It is years since I visited the place and I do not know if my father is still alive. I had thought him dead. The land is not mine but it was my childhood home, the place that contained and shaped me.

I remember it as it was, quarries and overgrown woodland, before it was cleared and levelled. I was the one who watched him clear and level it. I was the one who stood beside him.

There are two labourers working in a quarry a few yards from the path. I mumble a greeting but continue walking.

Then, rounding the bend at the bottom of the drive, I see him. He is standing beside Mr Shoemaker. Tiny, ancient Mr Shoemaker, possessor of but a single tooth.

He – I am speaking now of my father – has not changed. He is as he was when I last saw him, all those years ago. But the house, my father's house, is gone.

Sometimes we find something missing only to awake and find it not missing at all. We leave something somewhere and find it gone. But a house cannot disappear like a stage elephant. A house cannot be shielded from view by some obstacle in the line of sight or hidden by a series of reflective apparatuses. A house is made of bricks and mortar and cannot be moved. And besides, this was not just any house but the house of my father. A house of countless rooms and annexes.

The house could not have spread its wings and flown.

It occurred to me that perhaps I was dreaming but then I

My Father's House

remembered that we live inside our dreams and dreams are all we have.

My father desisted from his work (he and Mr Shoemaker were always hard at work) and looked up at me. His rosy face was smiling.

I notice a change, I said.

My father frowned.

The house. I opened my hands. The house has gone.

O, that, said my father, smiling again. That's nothing to worry about. It is being moved. It's a perfectly straightforward matter. You saw it in two, taking care not to damage the security chain on the front door, measure it up and reposition it. It is being moved so that it does not look directly onto the other house.

The other house? I was not aware there was another house. But then I thought – does he perhaps mean my brother's house?

The house is being moved. He smiled uncomprehendingly on and on. Moved so that it does not look directly onto the other house. And, he added, angled downwards.

A man in the prime of life bent over a fence with an implement in his hand beneath the burning sun. He has no care for the weather. He works his land in any weather, from burning sun to freezing rain. It is, under the circumstances, a wonder he survives.

A woman despatches me to find him. Has he fallen, or drowned in a ditch? No; there he is, halfway down a quarry with an implement in his hand.

Above the roar of thunder and lightning I shout down to him.

Are you alright?

He cannot hear, so engrossed is he in his work, so loud the roll and crash of the thunder and lightning.

I call again.

I give up. He can neither see nor hear me.

Dreams and Deceptions

Now he comes in, to hang his clothes to dry. He hangs them in a room at the side of the house, a small hot room which smells of oil and contains a boiler. His clothes are little more than rags. He hangs them to dry on a wooden frame beside the boiler. Then he emerges: naked, filthy. He walks through the kitchen leaving dark footprints behind him. He laughs when someone comments on his nakedness.

I was born naked and I will die naked, he says.

He is carrying a basket of logs. He carries the logs through the house until he comes to a room with a fireplace. He kneels before the fireplace to build a fire. He heaps kindling upon an unfolded newspaper – he has little interest in 'news', caring only for the news inside his own head – and strikes a match. He continues kneeling and gazing into the fireplace as the flames lick up in oval orange shapes, some large, some small, each containing within itself a blue diamond. The kindling takes light and begins to splutter and roar. It splutters now and roars like thunder. The pyrotechnist cackles with laughter. Then he constructs an edifice of wood upon the fire and rejoices as it burns.

Now he is sitting in an arm-chair (still filthy, still naked) one leg draped over the side of the chair gazing into the fire. He begins to talk to himself. One word at a time. Laughing, chattering to himself. A word, another word, three words. A peal of laughter. More words.

A young woman enters the room and addresses him.

You're disgusting, she says. And mad.

He looks up at her with bloodshot eyes.

Are you speaking to me?

You know perfectly well to whom I'm speaking. And you know what you are. Disgusting, mad.

He pulls her to him and attempts to smother her in kisses. She pulls away from him.

I'm not your sister, she says. Nor am I your dolly bird.

My Father's House

My father decides to cut down a wood. He employs a team of woodcutters to assist him. These men come stony-eyed equipped with chainsaws. At once they set about their business, applying the chainsaws to the great oaks and elms that the wood contains until they creak, groan, topple and fall.

At the very top of the tallest tree is a squirrels' drey.

My father kills these helpless squirrels with his bare hands, crushing their skulls till their eyes pop out.

A servant runs into the room where my father tears at my hair.

I cannot abide your kind, he says calmly.

A man in his mid-forties with stubble on his chin and calm brown eyes, one of which has a tendency to wander.

I am standing over him with my hat in my hand. All this is a dream though it is not a dream. It is, or was, my father's house.

Epithalamion, Tunis, August 1971

A girl of fourteen was being married to our friend's cousin, a moustachioed young man of twenty or so. The girl was beautiful. When she danced – one arm curled over her head, an enigmatic smile on her lips, her body rocking in a slow circle – she was graceful and beautiful beyond measure.

We sat in a corner, no-one quite knowing if we were honoured guests or ordinary guests, so placed to the side. The room was cavernous, filled with wedding guests and long trestle tables that would be loaded with food. Musicians, mostly drummers, played on a stage – looping and twisting rhythms on clay drums, dipping and soaring, twisting and turning, rhythms of the soul and the night. It seemed that the girl's main role was to dance. Various males, similar in appearance to the lucky groom, were allowed to dance with, or at least adjacent to, her – in front of her, around her, but not to touch her.

She danced, knowing every male eye in the room was upon her.

Except they weren't. The older generation of men – the ones with creased leathery faces, wide smiles, grey moustaches – didn't watch her at all.

She rocked back and forth, twining lengths of cloth around her, within her immaculate dance.

We sat with our friend, Jamael, and his family.

Isn't she beautiful, he said, smiling at me.

Yes, I said. Your cousin is a lucky man.

Food was produced, gallons of it – vast vats of meat in spiced sauces, vegetables, seaweed, sweets, spicy and lustrous delicacies,

Epithalamion, Tunis, August 1971

borne by dark-eyed serving girls. None of us would go hungry tonight. I asked Jamael,
 How long does this go on for?
 The epithalamion? Two days and two nights.
 Two days and nights? And no-one sleeps?
 Well, yes. A little sleep of course.
 And, er, the bride? Does she sleep? Or does she just dance?
 She just dances. Until they are tied.
 Tied?
 By a rope. Then he carries her off. That is the end of the epithalamion.

Jasmine was chatting away to some of the women.
 Will we get a chance to meet her? I asked.
 Sure, said Jamael. He turned and whistled at the girl. She stopped dancing and walked over to us, hips swaying, smiling. All fourteen years of her. Stopped in front of us. Brown eyes looking straight into mine.
 My cousin, Jenna. My friends from England, Charlie and Jasmine.
 Jenna went on smiling. She acknowledged us with her eyes, gave a sort of half curtsy but did not speak.
 Isn't she beautiful?
 Yes. Jenna, I said, you dance beautifully.
 Her brown eyes turned questioningly to Jamael. Her smile didn't falter. He translated and she said something back.
 She says she is sure you too dance beautifully.
 I laughed. No. Tell her she is like a dream. Like a princess from the middle ages.
 The middle ages?
 A long time ago.
 He translated. This time she had the grace to blush slightly and lower her eyes.
 She says, she is lucky to be marrying a good man.

Fuck, I said – no don't translate that. Tell her I hope he is a good man. I hope she is happy.

He translated. This time she looked straight at me, still smiling.

She says thank you and she hopes you too will be happy.

She said something quickly, half under her breath, to Jamael, then went back to the centre of the room, lifted her curved arm and, in the second before she began to dance, enveloped me with her eyes. It was like sailing into the stars. Then she began to rock, her arm fluted above her head, smiling, turning, first this way, then that.

We went back through the late night streets to the hotel. Night was observed mainly in the breach in this part of Tunis. Young men rode motor scooters, klaxons blaring; young girls jumped on and off them, laughing; music pounded from a disco.

Can you believe it?

What, getting married at fourteen?

Looking like that.

She was fourteen!

No, she wasn't.

I thought of her standing there smiling while they tied her to her new owner, the moustachioed young man, and then turning her dark eyes to him. Just standing there. Like a fucking birthday present. He was a lucky man. And he knew it. At least he should have done.

Yes she was, she said.

No she wasn't. And she wasn't a virgin either.

Of course she was, said Jasmine laughing.

We were tired. Disco music pounded up through the floorboards of our bedroom.

Trust us to pick a fucking hotel with a disco in it.

She rolled round in the bed, naked and sleepy, and kissed me.

There, she said. Better?

Epithalamion, Tunis, August 1971

Jamael wanted to come to England to study, which was why he'd befriended us. I had some crazy fantasy that maybe she could come too. Music pounded up through the floorboards with an insane persistence that perfectly matched the technology that produced it.
    Boom boom boom. Thud thud thud.
    Fuck this, I said.
    We can change hotels tomorrow.
    Yes, I said. We will.
    Goodnight, sweetheart. I leaned across and kissed her.

The Rough-Legged Buzzard

My childhood was dominated by the presence (and absence) of a rough-legged buzzard. On Saturdays, when my father had me, he would sometimes take me to the Western Rockies to scout for birds. My father was very interested in birds, especially raptors – his favourites were kestrels and eagles but he loved all raptors, especially the scarcer ones. Perhaps he saw something of himself in them. He loved songbirds too, and pretty finches, and kingfishers and swans and herons, but would not go out of his way for them as he would for raptors. He went to the eastern marches to see marsh harriers and to Scotland for eagles and ospreys and hen harriers. He went to the Western Rockies mainly, I think, in the hope of seeing a peregrine though we never saw one. On the Saturdays he had me, he took me.

I never wanted to go. I would wail and kick and make a great fuss. On the way to the Rockies was a playbarn where children could play on inflatable slides and climbing frames and, a little way past that, a leisure centre with a swimming pool; even as a tiny child I loved swimming. So my father would say, We'll take a picnic to the Rockies and on the way back we can go to the playbarn or the pool. Deal? I would kick up a great fuss – No, I don't want to go to the Rockies, I want to go straight to the playbarn! – but in the end he would get his way. Sometimes he would get quite angry. Who's driving the car? Who's paying for all this? But he wouldn't be angry for long and if he was I would cry and apologise and tell him I wanted everything to be alright again. That made him feel bad and so it would.

We would take a picnic come rain or shine. He would make sandwiches or, if we were in a rush, as we often were, buy sausage rolls (later I became a vegetarian but that's another story). He would make ginger beer out of apple and ginger juice and sparkling water and he would always add a small cake or a bar of chocolate. On the way we would talk. I would ask him questions, about my mother or about his childhood, and he would always answer, truthfully I think. He was careful not to lie for he did not want to fill me with lies. Or we would listen to music – he had a cassette player in his car and many cassettes, mostly country-style music by women singers. I used to sing along to some of them. I learned not just the tunes and the words but the phrasing – though some of the singers could do things with their voices I could never do. Sometimes he played music I didn't like, dreary wailing music that hurt my ears, and I would block my ears until he took it off. Why don't you like it? he would say, quite crossly. It's real music. But it wasn't real music to me, just dreary wailing. It's too grown up for you, he would say, and gaze through the windscreen looking for birds.

Looking for birds: it was a feature, maybe the feature of my childhood. What's that? he would say, as a black bird flew across our vision. Crow? No, that was a jackdaw. What's that? Buzzard? Buzzard! Good. Well done. I learned the names of many birds – crows, jackdaws, buzzards, kites, as well as the garden birds, robins, blackbirds, blue tits, wrens, and some of the river birds, swans, herons, kingfishers.

Then it would begin to rain. It rained a lot in the Western Rockies. The rain would splatter on the windscreen, the wipers would come on, splish splash splatter. Sometimes it stopped and sometimes it didn't. Sometimes when we arrived (we always went to the same place, a small empty nature reserve capped with a high mountain) it was raining, sometimes the rain had eased off. Sometimes there was sun, at other times snow. It didn't matter to my father. Right, he would say, here we are. Can we have lunch in the car? No, he would say, don't be ridiculous. We haven't come all this way just to sit in the car. So out we'd get, or out he'd get and I wouldn't, until he came up with some threat or bribe I couldn't ignore. He would put on his boots, sling his binoculars round his neck, lift me up and plonk me down in the open hatch at the back to put on my boots, put on his rucksack, grasp his stick, check everything three times and lock the car. And off we would go.

My father and I. I remember him as though it were yesterday, with his big waterproof jacket, his muddy trousers, his green boots, a rucksack on his back, a stick in his hand, binoculars. And me, less than half his size, dressed in a padded floral coat with a bobble hat on my head and my little boots on my little feet beside him. Or behind him. Wait for me! I would wail. Sometimes he would wait, sometimes he wouldn't. Sometimes he would march on ahead. Sometimes he would stop, raise the binoculars to his eyes and scan for birds. Scanning as I reached him, panting, on the hillside. Ravens, he might say. Or buzzards. Or, lowering his binoculars, nothing at all. There weren't many birds in the Western Rockies – no robins or blackbirds, that I saw anyway, no pretty finches. Just scattered trees, high mountains and miles of moorland. Empty for the most part.

I want to go home.

It wasn't far to our picnic place, less than a mile anyway. Along a stony path, steep in places, through scrubby trees, to a stone wall. In the wall was a gate but beside the gate there was gap in the wall, a stone you could sit on linking the two parts of the wall. It can't have been very effective in terms of keeping stock in or out but we never saw any stock. Just miles of moorland and the high rocky mountain and the stream and, sometimes, birds. We would cross the wall – my father opening and closing the gate, I skipping through the gap, over the stone – and there, on a little bank beside the gate, where the path forked, we would have our picnic. Cold usually, raining often, but sometimes, once in a while, the sun shining. My father would sit on the bank and I beside him. He would unsling his rucksack and take out the food. And we would eat. It was then that he saw it.

What's that? he said. I could see nothing. There! He was

The Rough-Legged Buzzard

pointing to a tree about a hundred yards away. Still I could see nothing. He found it with the binoculars. That's something, he said, to the abstract air. He handed me the binoculars. Still I could see nothing. He took the binoculars back, looked through them again. That's definitely something. What is it? I said. I don't know, he said. Then it flew.

I could see it.

He followed the bird with his binoculars. That's something. Definitely something. It's not a buzzard. It's too big for a buzzard.

Then, most startling of all, after hanging for a moment in the air, the huge bird began to hover.

It's hovering, he said.

I am four years old now. Not literally – I was four years old then. But I am four years old now in my memory. I am not me. Or perhaps I am. Either way. There he was, has he gone? I don't know. I don't know what's true or false anymore or what anything means.

It's hovering.

The bird stopped hovering, glided into a tree and sat there.

What was it? I said.

I don't know, my father said. It looks like a buzzard but it isn't a buzzard. It's too big, it's got a pale head and it hovers. Buzzards don't hover.

Is it a peregrine? (I knew my father loved peregrines.)

No, he said. Peregrines have black moustaches. It doesn't have a black moustache. And peregrines don't hover.

He ran through all the possibilities – marsh harrier, no, they don't hover, kestrel, too big for a kestrel, goshawk, too big for a goshawk and they don't hover either.

Finally he said, Perhaps it's a rough-legged buzzard.

We spent the whole afternoon watching it, or rather my father did. I played in the stream and fell over and got muddy and burst into tears. Stop crying, he said, as though it were my fault. Every second Saturday, the Saturdays he had me, we would go back to

Dreams and Deceptions

look for the rough-legged buzzard. But we never saw it again. Most days it was raining. One day it was raining so heavily we had our picnic in an unlocked church, facing each other across a long wooden table, dripping wet and freezing cold. Every year we went back, five, six, seven, looking for the rough-legged buzzard but we never saw it again. I don't know where it went, how long it lived or where its home was.

Helene

This place, I tell them, is the centre of the alternative universe.
Perhaps the universe doesn't have a centre? says Helene, who has been speaking non-stop since I entered but in such a whispery voice that no-one can hear what she is saying.
Monty, who is as deaf as I am, pauses for a moment, a bag of plums in his hand.
The alternative universe does, and this is it. Isn't it, Monty?
O yes, says Monty. Very much so. Only the other day
It is all around us, whispers Helene, smiling. I notice three things about Helene: she is quite pretty (though very pale); she looks stressed; she is longer young.
It's a metaphor. The universe doesn't have a geographical centre
I was saying, only the other day, says Monty, in the Post Office
We are tiny, tiny, says Helene. Tiny. In the overall scheme.
O no, I say, we are not. We are huge, vast. In fact, we are the universe, each one of us. Take a look out there, at Castle Street. Do you see all that stuff out there? Well, close your eyes and it's gone. Nothing. Nada. There is no universe apart from our perception of it. When we die, it ceases to exist.
O no, says Monty, I don't want to be responsible for that. For the end of the universe.
Well, you will be. We won't, will we, Helene?, but Monty will.
Only in this town could we be having this conversation in the greengrocer's, says Monty, who is himself a greengrocer.
O I don't know. It would be quite normal for, say, Marrakesh.
There you go, says Monty. Normal for Marrakesh.
You are very arrogant, whispers Helene, smiling.

Dreams and Deceptions

Do you live here?

I am living here six months, she whispers. To renew my energy levels. My energy levels have become depleted. She smiles in a slightly mad way.

And what do you do?

I write.

O – what do you write?

I write, smiles Helene.

Poetry?

I never talk about my writing, smiles Helene.

Where then is the edge of the universe? The edge of the universe, I explain, is on the other side of the river, about half a mile, heading east.

And what lies beyond the edge of the universe?'

Fields and sheds and cows. Or not. Whatever you see when you stand at the edge of the universe and look. Perhaps nothing.

There is no such thing as nothing, whispers Helene. Only force fields of energy.

She is leaving. Light tremulous steps towards the door, clutching her bag of plums. She holds out her hand.

Helene.

James. If you like, I'll meet you down by the river tonight at seven and show you the edge of the universe.

Okay, whispers Helene.

Three Suicides

The word 'suicide' ('murder of self') is presumed to be a sixteenth or seventeenth century invention; prior to that terms such as 'self-murder' or 'murder by his (or her) own hand' were used. Attitudes towards suicide varied widely; by some it was considered a noble (and quite rational) ending; by others, a sin against society or God.

God made us and, intrinsic within us, is the time and manner of our deaths (perhaps). As for society, society needs the strong more than the weak. And yet suicide is not necessarily a weakness.

> Mr Renard took the train
> In the rain
> Wound up on the southern plain
> Walked across the southern hill
> And spilled himself into the sea;
> Had he wings he would have flown
> Had he love he would have known
> Love of God is higher than
> Love of woman or of man.

Can animals commit suicide? Almost certainly. Animals will fast to death, allow themselves to die, make their way into the undergrowth to die. It is a strange delusion that animals have no awareness of death. They have awareness of two things only – life and death. Life is all around them, within the insects that plague and pester them, the birds that torment them, the fish that bounce out of the water and fly towards them. Life too in the wind that blows cold in winter, hot in summer, in the hay

Dreams and Deceptions

feed or the muzzle bag that sustains them (some animals spend most of their waking hours eating), even in the rocks and stones, even in the earth, even in the house that houses them. But death is also all around them. The death of their comrades, their fellow-travellers, their fellow-sufferers, their fellow-victims: accidental or deliberate, for some animals are reared for the sole purpose of being put to death and eaten (such is the 'great hunger').

The second suicide was that of a young girl. She died twice, once in 1976 and once in 2014. Almost a lifetime apart. The first time she opened a gas oven, tried to gas herself and failed. Was she on her knees? Did she lie flat, did she crawl? Did she kneel? Did she think of how she would be found, of who would find her? What went through her mind? She was twenty-four. In the end she opened the window and rolled out into the night. Did she imagine God would save her (as he saved Mr Renard)? Did she think nobody loved her? And what if they didn't, why do we need love so? Of course, we are not what (who) we think we are. We are part of a whole. We have a need to re-embrace the whole, become 'one' again. Was it that she couldn't face the night? She died instantly (perhaps) at or around midnight. Her lover had told her that he didn't love her. That he wanted to be her friend, not her lover. Not even her special friend. Just 'a friend'. A soft let-down (he thought). Then he left. They were probably a little drunk, a little high.

The third suicide, the 'other' suicide, was thirty-eight years later. This time she had lived her life, had had a 'career' (a strangely unstable word to describe what it describes), had married, borne children, suffered doubts and disappointments, sung in public, written books, yet still felt strangely unsure of herself; as though the love that had been withheld, all those years ago, still possessed the power to reduce her achievements to nothing.

Everything is nothing in the eyes of God. There is no achievement that is any greater than the crook of God's little finger; yet even that crook, that misshapen command, is unsure of itself, incomplete, less than redemptive. All her life she had waited with death as her constant companion. That night in 1976, when God saved her, was the only day in her life that mattered; what happened in between (her career, her marriage, her children) was just part of the waiting. Then God called her unexpectedly. She had completed the third book of a trilogy and was ready to send it to the publisher. She told everyone what she was about to do. She went to the Post Office, posted the typescript, returned home and hanged herself.

She hanged herself from the stairs. Her husband found her. He was also a writer and so perhaps more able to rationalise it. Though perhaps not; perhaps he too sought answers where there were none. She was dead, the world moves on. The sun doesn't stop turning. The sun only stops turning when we are alive, and then only for a moment (a moment so short as to be, to science anyway, immeasurable). Yet long enough for union with God.

I never said goodbye, Mr Renard, but I remember you: tousle-haired, wearing light brown cords, addressing the landlord as 'mine host', drinking beer with your arm upon the bar, reading your poems in 'small rooms' to 'other poets', believing in yourself, believing in your life; then, when life did not match your dreams, believing instead in death. I remember you taking the train to the southern plain, clambering high upon the southern cliffs, spreading your wings to fly. Goodbye dear sister, I remember you too – not crawling, not walking, but flying towards the gas oven as though you couldn't wait to get there, finding death there, the death that in my dreams eluded you. We are all of us unfulfilled. Life and death are simple things, they do not matter.

Badu Badula

I am rocking to and fro on the brown wicker chair. The air is grey and filled with colour. There is a motion of life and it is like a many-coloured stream or coat and sounds too, like the sounds of wind over rocks, though not violent, no more violent than

everything in its place, at the same time, the time of encapsulation, looking through the wrong end of a telescope and everything encapsulated into one, nothing, in its place, the amoeba splitting randomly, every movement bizarre and different then, before the new could even be understood, another, imperfection gliding into perfection before returning to

    Fuck, says Badu. Fuckfuckfuckfuckfuck. His eyes crossed staring at a point   rocking gently, rhythmically, his paws folded upon his belly   fuck fuckfuckfuckfuckfuck. Fuck

Cars pass within a few feet of where he is sitting. Buses too, big red buses, nosing in and out, vying with pedestrians who cross before them or stand and wait or enter and leave. Jaws like sharks sucking in spewing out. There are worlds in which nothing happens, many of them. Too many to count, thinks Badu, only is what is right here and beyond nothing

    Fuckfuckfuck. He is quite tired now with his rocking. His rocking might put him to sleep or back further, into the womb, where he once was, perfectly happy. Until he outgrew the womb. Ten thousand miles away the universe expands every second light travels to the furthest and back again

Fuckfuckfuck. He is tiring of the game. Fuck! Like duck, suck or quack. Fuck! Fuck! The observer cannot observe himself. It is necessary to draw attention to himself. Fuck! he cries

Two men are there, moving empty paper cups. One, the taller, smiles at him; cocks his head, opens his hands. Wanting, or asking, something. He nods. The man gathers the empty paper cups finds one that contains water. He holds it out to him. He shakes his head. His teeth are smiling. The man smiles again, replaces the water on the table. The other man stands with his head cocked to the side looking down at the ground. He holds in his hand a plastic bag from which protrudes the edge of a board. The first man goes on smiling and gathering. Then he tells the other man to wait and goes

He has gone. Somehow he has been silenced. He was saying 'fuck' over and over but now has been silenced. The same people are moving along the same street in the same direction and the same buses opening their jaws to gorge and disgorge, the crowd grows neither bigger nor smaller but remains the same, fat thin young old all colours shapes black and white fat and thin tall and small   he sees nothing at all   with his crossed eyes

The tall man, the man with the hat, has returned and is speaking to the small man. The small man clutches his bag and says nothing. He would close his eyes, perhaps even sleep, but his eyes cannot close. Nor focus. He thinks perhaps he will resume saying 'fuck' but realises he has been silenced. The tall man has moved the paper cups the overflowing ashtray and gone away now he returns bearing cups of hot liquid. Tea. Hot chocolate. He pulls a newspaper from his bag and begins shuffling through the paper,

Dreams and Deceptions

separating sections, putting some in one pile, some in another. He will wait. His name is Badu Badula. He has been waiting a long time and will continue to wait. He lifts his great head and stares across the table at the tall man who shuffles the papers. He tries to focus his eyes up to a point

The man has separated his newspapers. He holds out his hands and speaks.
Paper? he says.
Paper, thinks Badu Badula. An expression crosses his face like a shadow. His face, his eyes, his legs, all crossed. Like an amoeba upon a slide, sliding, separating. One of the papers, the glossiest and most colourful, catches his eye (the one that is at that moment focussed). He looks at the paper then at the man then beckons with his finger. The man smiles.
This one?
Badu Badula stretches out his great paw and seizes the papers. The glossy colourful one and several others at once. He puts them on the table in front of him. He looks at the man and opens his great maw to show his teeth and gums.
You like reading?
Plenty.
Badu laughs. His laugh is surprisingly light merry and high-pitched. Not the belly rumble you might expect. His laugh is surprisingly light merry and high-pitched. Badu has never read anything in his life. He cannot read. But he likes the idea of reading. And perhaps, should he like the idea long enough, long enough and hard enough, it will become real and he Badu will be able to read and be back in the womb where he belongs.

Life is short, he says, and laughs again.
O yes, says the man. And filled with pain.
Badu roars with laughter rocks to and fro upon his wicker chair. All around there are sounds, cars, buses, motorbikes, the

loud wailing and screeching of the fat and the thin, the women and the men. Badu neither hears nor cares. Life is filled with pain. The tall man has described it perfectly.

Irene

He stabs the map with his finger. The sun beyond the window stills for a moment and unleashes unimagined rays, brightening the red mountains, till their very redness sings and the world is other.
 The world is a beautiful place, she sighs. I never knew it was so beautiful. And you, what do you do?
 Walk.
 Steve drives. Steve likes to drive everywhere. Don't you, Steve?
 Not everywhere, says Steve.
 I am a drama teacher. Or was. I still work part-time. I teach college students mostly, kids who want to learn. They are the best to teach. Steve is retired.
 She looks out of the window, at the singing mountains and the small fluttering birds and the larger birds that fly slowly back and forth across the face of the mountain.
 Our children are grown up now. The eldest, Steve, is, like his father, a dentist. Our daughter, Daphne, a biologist; she has escaped to the wastes of the north. Soon she will be having children of her own. I will be a grandmother. She laughs. Funny that. I am not sure I'm ready to be a grandmother. We took early retirement. Funny to think of it now, Steve and Irene
 You are Irene?
 O no, I am not Irene.
 She gazes through the window as the sun resumes its laborious journey and shadows cross the mountain, first slight and high, then descending, until the entire mountain is in shadow.

Irene

Here, says Steve, jabbing with his finger. These are ruins? Right here!

He looks. He has never seen these ruins or, if he has, he has not remembered them. But they are there, sure enough, a few yards from the ruined chapel. Converted into a byre, most likely, or a picnic area, though picnic areas are few and far between on these islands.

He studies the map. He finds the ruined chapel, the ruined village by the coast, and Steve's ruins.

Yes, he says.

They are far from here?

No. Just a couple of minutes away.

That's it! cries Steve. He bundles up the map and turns to his wife. A couple of minutes. Then an hour to the ruined village and an hour back. And then we drive.

Take a day, he says.

O no, says Steve. We only have a week. We want to see everything in a week.

You can't see everything in a week.

The door opens and Mr Begood enters. He stares first at Steve and Irene, if she is Irene, then at him. He has finished his breakfast, the empty cups and plates lie scattered and discarded upon the table. He begins to move towards him

Steve says,

Ruins. And more ruins. Your country is full of ruins. Ours is full of bears. They come in the night and eat out of the dustbins. It gets so bad marksmen have to be brought in. Gunfire up and down Main Street. But it's only bears. And then their carcases are taken away for recycling. Isn't that right, Irene?

Don't listen to him, says Irene. It happened once, it hasn't happened since. When the snow was bad in the north and bears started rooting around in the town.

Have you finished? says Mr Begood.

Yes, he says.

Dreams and Deceptions

Enjoy your day
Steve rolls up his map. Irene rises.
Hope to meet you again. We will be back.
You can never go back, he says. He tells her of his American and Canadian ancestry, his mother's aunt who lived in Canada. Come visit us anytime, she says, we aren't hard to find. Main Street and bears, says Steve. You can't miss it.

Problems

Not a problem.
It was obviously her job to say this over and over again.
Not a problem.
But of course it all went wrong.

That could be a problem, she said.
What could be a problem?
The last bit.
What did I say?
You said 'You sometimes took credit card details by email' she said.
Yes. But I delete them immediately, he lied.
Not a problem, she said.
Is it a problem or isn't it a problem?
Is what a problem? she said.
The fact that I take them and delete them.
Yes, she said.
Yes what?
Yes, that is a problem. Though in another way it is not a problem.
You mean it is a problem with a solution?
Yes, she said. You need to go online and answer some questions. You could have your advisor with you, to help you.
How many questions?
Two thousand eight hundred.
Two thousand eight hundred?
Yes.
And then?
Then we would have to say, It is not a problem.

Dreams and Deceptions

I could spend the rest of my life answering your questions.
Not a problem.
Why not?
Because it isn't. Life is short.
Is life short?
Life is short. Terminally short. We are all fallen.
No we aren't, he said.
Speak for yourself, she said.
Why? he said.
Not a problem.
Have you ever got wet. Like truly wet?
Yes.
When?
When I was a child in county Kildare.
Was that a problem?
No.
So why so this such a great problem?
It isn't, she said. Just answer the questions. Then you might
No.
No.
No. I have enough problems.
No-one has enough problems.
Problems have solutions.
Not always.
Are you from county Kildare?
Yes.
Is that a problem?
No.
I don't have time, he said.
I do, she said.

It was. It isn't now.
Do you really love me?
No, she said.
Is that a problem?

The line went dead.

The Neighbour's Wife

He cleaned and oiled the weapon, the smell of oil on his hands, scoured the barrel, hung it on the rack. He went in for supper. His wife said,

Where have you been with your oily hands?

Out, he said.

Your hands are oily and your shirt too. You are covered in oil.

So what, he said.

So this is a nice table. A clean table.

I've been shooting game.

Game? You call those tiny creatures game?

They are game, he said. Anything you shoot is game.

Anything you shoot is game, said his wife. She placed his dinner, which she'd kept warm under the grill, upon the table. I'm going upstairs, she said. On second thoughts I'm going out.

She went out onto the veranda and smoked a cigarette. She gazed across the unkempt lawn towards the garden belonging to their neighbour, the neighbour she had never seen. He had seen them once: a dishevelled man with a wife half his age. Unlike his own wife who, although younger, seemed older than him. His neighbour's wife was young and attractive, despite the neighbour's appearance: an old green coat with military buttons, a beer-gut, lank hair that hung down over his neck and onto his shoulders. They had stepped out at the same moment. He had caught the man's eye. Both were carrying guns.

Neighbour, he said.

The man just gave him a twisted look, a look that unnerved him. He said nothing more, watched as the man walked down his

Dreams and Deceptions

driveway to his pick-up, loaded the gun, climbed in and drove away. The neighbour's wife came and stood on the path vacated by the neighbour. Half his age: young enough to be his daughter, wearing a short skirt and a top that appeared to have nothing apart from the neighbour herself beneath it.

Hi, she said. I'm Karen.
Hi.
Who are you?
Me? Dave.
Dave, she said.
Yes.
Well, good to meet you, Dave.

She turned and walked back in knowing he was watching her. Nothing, he sensed, beneath her skirt or her top. He had never seen her before. As she reached the house she turned, threw him a smile, then went inside and closed the door.

I'm going shooting, he said, and kissed her on the lips. Or tried to kiss her on the lips: she turned her head at the last minute and he kissed not her lips but the side of her nose.

Go, she said. Go and shoot your game.
All animals are game, he said.

He climbed into his pick-up and drove out of the driveway into light traffic. He turned on the radio but there was nothing on, just country music and dinner jazz. Country music was sorrow with a smile on its face, not his cup of tea at all. Dinner jazz was better but not the sort of jazz he would choose. He would rather listen to Coltrane or Miles Davies, something with life in it, not the lifeless passivity of dinner jazz. Jazz designed not to offend – but, like everything else designed not to offend, all it did was offend. There are two types of people in this world, he thought, the ones who do what they please and the ones who spend their lives trying not to offend. Trying not to offend: what sort of insanity is that?

The Neighbour's Wife

He stopped at a red light and a police car drew up behind him. He wasn't concerned. He had a license for his gun, he was clean, there was nothing wrong with the pick-up, not unless they wanted to find something wrong. But with the police you never can tell. Sometimes they weren't interested: other times they'd stop you for nothing. The women were the worst. At least with a man you could talk to him, man to man. You can't talk to a man-hating woman wearing a badge.

As the lights changed the police lights went on and he swore under his breath. Nothing for it. He pulled over. The police vehicle stopped behind him at a distance of half a dozen car lengths. 'Step out of your vehicle' came a loud distorted voice though there was no-one to be seen.

He considered for five seconds. There are stories: gunmen disguised as police officers who will gun down you as soon as you step out. There are some strange people in the world. After five seconds reflection he opened the door and stepped out of his vehicle. 'Flat on the ground with your hands behind your head' came the voice. Now he knew he was in trouble.

He had only met his neighbour's wife once...this is a lie. He had only *known* her once. He had met her three times. The first time, the second time and the third time. The first time she'd stood on the driveway wearing nothing but a loose top and a short skirt and told him her name was Karen. The second time he had found her gardening beside the fence that separated their properties wearing a bikini top and an even shorter skirt. Her husband's pick-up was not on the driveway and her husband was nowhere to be seen. Where his own wife was he could only guess: sitting upstairs in front of the mirror, maybe, muttering incantations.

Hello again.

Karen paused from her gardening, looked up and smiled. She was barefoot and not wearing any make-up. She stood up.

O hi, she said.

Nice day.

Dreams and Deceptions

I thought I'd do some gardening. Catch the sun. What do you think?

What do I think?

She smiled. He imagined her reaching behind her back, untying her bikini top and letting it fall to the ground. Not that much was left to the imagination. Her breasts were mostly visible: loose, white, above average size; soft, inviting. Inviting: is that what women's breasts are? Do they invite? He guessed they did. We've all been there, he thought, except those of us weaned from bottles.

Yes, she said, what do you think?

I think – he smiled and glanced at the sky. I think it is a nice day to catch the sun.

Yes, she said. O my! She hopped up on one foot. O damn!

What's happened?

A thorn. In my foot. Yikes! She hopped about on one foot whilst trying to lift the other with her hands. Can you help?

Sure, he said. His neighbour's wife sat on the grass while he examined her foot. There was no thorn. O, she said, I could have sworn there was! Was she a nymphomaniac?

He would not fall for it again. The last time was bad enough: flat on the ground with his hands behind his neck then strip-searched and roughed up at the local police station. Nothing he could do: the police are a law unto themselves. In some countries that isn't the case. In some countries, like, say, Sweden, the police are polite and respectful. They don't gun you down from thirty feet because you twitched whilst placing your hands behind your head. Everyone has a choice, he thought, the choices keep occurring, they come and go so swiftly most of the time you don't notice them. But this one he noticed. He had a choice but no time to make it. The sun was as high and warm as the day he sat on his neighbour's lawn attending to his neighbour's wife's foot. She had asked him to come in to clean his hands, to have a coffee and smoke a cigarette. He'd barely touched the coffee and was only half way through the cigarette when she'd reached behind her back and untied her bikini top. That's better, she'd said. Were her breasts inviting? Enough-to-drive-a-man-insane inviting. The butcher, the baker and the candlestick maker.

He threw himself back into his vehicle, grabbed the gun, kicked open the door on the passenger side and started firing. Bang bang. The first bullet missed, the second shattered the windscreen of the police vehicle. The vehicle began to wail. A side door opened and shots were returned. Now, he thought, surprisingly calmly, we are engaged in a gun battle. What is the first rule of gun battles? Do not retreat. And the second? Do not stop firing. That's it: stand your ground and keep firing. Advance if you must. The policewoman (it was, as he'd surmised, a woman) must have had the same idea. They advanced towards each other, firing steadily, until at last she went down. She had a hole in the side of her face the size of a small rabbit. Surprisingly she was still alive. He had one bullet left and could think of no better place for it than the policewoman's brain. Now she will have no brain, at least not a functioning one.

They fucked there and then on the sitting room sofa. She was passionate, more passionate than any woman he had ever encountered. Gasping, grabbing, tearing at his hair. Coming before he did (which was better than the other way round). Afterwards she was not passionate. She was cool and collected. She put her skirt back on but remained topless while he finished his cigarette. She kissed him on the lips as he left, standing on tiptoe in her bare feet. About ten seconds later her husband returned, swinging his pick-up into the driveway, carrying a dead deer.

He drove on to the hunting woods but somehow his heart wasn't in it. In fact his heart was right out of it. He thought of the dead policewoman's face and the dead deer carried by his neighbour's husband. Will I ever see her again? Probably not. The sun was

Dreams and Deceptions

warming the earth, it was summer, that made it worse: worst time to have the blues is on a hot day in summer. A hot still day in summer with no-one around. No-one around: that was his clue. There is no-one around, no-one to see what I do or what I don't do.

Budapest

They sit in the train. Peddlers come with coffee and biscuits. He smiles at her. She smiles at him.
    Our lives together, he says.
    Our lives together.
    She turns her head as the train begins to move. But it's the neighbouring train, not theirs, that is moving.
    Hard to tell which train is moving.
    She leans her head against the back of the cushioned seat and closes her eyes. She started the journey with one man and now she is with another. And before that there was another
    Is he really there? Am I really here?
    She opens her eyes and sees him

    When I was a child
    She stops.
    Yes?
    I used to watch my mother sewing. She sewed and sewed. Really she sewed her life away.
    And your father?
    She turns back to the window.
    And your father? he persists.
    No, she says.

She was a teacher in New York. Her closest friend was another teacher, a black man. He was friendly, intelligent, a good teacher and kept himself in shape. All he had for breakfast was an apple. An apple and some water. Your body needs time to adjust. No coffee, nothing like that. Just a single apple.

Dreams and Deceptions

The fruit of the tree of knowledge.
Yes. He was a good man, she says.
What became of him?
He left.
Why?
I don't know.

Their train begins to move. They fall silent as the train pulls out of the station, rolls almost silently through the suburbs of the city then picks up speed as it reaches the countryside. They won't travel far on the train. They will alight before the border.

Peddlers come with coffee and biscuits. They don't have much money. Cheaper to buy coffee and biscuits on the road, in some village or roadside shack. Money doesn't matter. They won't go hungry. He is nineteen years old with blue eyes, curly brown hair and an embryonic beard. Like Christ, she thinks, only younger. She is smaller than him, a little overweight, with a pretty face, freckles and full lips. He has kissed those lips he doesn't know how many times since they met. We met on the road, he thinks, now we're travelling the road. And then? But the road never ends. The only true life is on the road.
   The only true life is on the road.
   I know, she says.
   Will you go back to New York?
   Not if I can help it.

They get a lift on a tractor lumbering through the Bulgarian countryside. The driver, a small dark man with a graceless leer, is eating plums. He offers them. He takes one and bites into it. The plum is alive with maggots. Where once there was a stone now there is only a wriggling mass of white maggots.
   Maggots, he says, spitting them out into a handkerchief.
   The driver smiles at him.

No good?

They're full of fucking maggots.

The driver shrugs. She stares out of the window at endless cornfields. The tractor lumbers on.

They get a lift with a fat Lebanese in a chauffeur-driven Mercedes. They sit in the back. The Lebanese tells them he is an ambassador. Do you have visas? They do not. Don't worry, he says. I will get you through. It is easy. When they reach the border the guards ask them for their passports. They do not have visas. The guards do not care about the visas, only bakshish. The ambassador speaks to them in German and hands them cigars the size of nuclear missiles. The guards wave them through.

See, is easy, he tells them. All they care about is – he rubs the middle finger of his right hand against his thumb.

Where are you staying in Budapest?

We don't know, he says.

You can stay at the Hilton, says the ambassador.

He wonders for a moment if the ambassador is planning to accommodate them.

Maybe, he says.

Before they reach the Hilton, in the centre of Budapest, there is a park. Drop us here, he says. They get out of the car, climb over the railings and sleep in the park.

They are heading west though they do not know it or at least are not fully reconciled to it.

It makes no sense to head west.

I know, she says.

The action is the other way. He points east.

I know, she says, looking at him with dark fathomless eyes.

They get a lift to Vienna. Before they reach Vienna they stop at a petrol station. They walk behind the petrol station and sleep in a field. Next morning they hitchhike the last few miles into

Dreams and Deceptions

Vienna. They sit in a coffee shop in the centre of Vienna with their rucksacks on the ground beside them.

When I was in Norway, he says, I sat in a café like this. I had no money, none at all. I asked for bread and water. They threw me out. The waiter actually took my chair from under me and stood brandishing it like a trident whilst pointing with his other hand down the street.

I thought you could sit in any café anywhere in the world and ask for a glass of water, she said.

Not in that one.

What were you doing in Norway?

I went fishing in a fjord. The boat got tangled up in fishing nets. We were stranded on an island for three nights and days. We only had one cassette – Forever Changes. We listened to it over and over again. I must know every word of every song.

When they reach England he leaves her in a hostel in London while he borrows a car and drives to Edinburgh. He has a girl in Edinburgh he hasn't seen for six months. They sit on the hillside halfway up Arthur's Seat while tears roll slowly down her cheeks.

It'll be like you never came back, she says.

His car packs up and he swaps it for a minivan. He drives back to London and picks her up from the hostel. They buy some hashish and drive west to St Ives. For two nights they sleep in the minivan. They find a holiday apartment in St Ives where they live for three weeks, writing songs and poems and making love. Every night they get high. After three weeks he is restless again. It seems to him their relationship is going nowhere. They should have turned back, gone east. Now that America is so close she is restless too.

Maybe I ought to go home, she says.
Okay.
You don't mind?
No.
Will you come?

Budapest

She will fly to America and he will follow. But will he? It is not her star he is following but his own. He has no idea where it will lead. He takes her to the airport, kisses her goodbye. She clings to him.
Promise you'll come.
Okay.
Is that a promise?
He doesn't reply. She pulls him tighter. If you don't come, I'll come for you. Planes don't wait, he says. She looks up at him, brushes a tear from her eye. I'll write. I'll write every day. And she does, every day, packages containing gifts – hand-knitted scarves, socks, hats – and love notes.

The Island

The sun pours down upon the sand like melted honey. In front of him the blue water sparkles with light, turning into bubbles of white spray as it hits the sand and retreats, uncertainly, as though it too were made semi-inert by the heat. The sky is blue and almost cloudless, like a veil that cannot hide the sun. He squints upwards: the sun's light is too bright and strong to bear.

He is six foot, slim and bony, with broad shoulders: an ironic contrast to the brain he cannot still, that moves at times almost at the speed of light, at other times disappears into caverns that open without warning, rendering him speechless and unable to factor even the simplest equation: he who once topped a nation-wide poll for child mathematical geniuses in the land of his birth. His genius was such that when his brain stopped working it did not simply stop but reversed itself, undid all the good it had achieved and became utterly alien. Thus it was that he performed the acts he performed entirely without thinking: as though he did not perform them but they performed themselves. He, his tall angular body, his beak-shaped nose, the locks of brown hair that fell across his forehead, merely the instrument.

There are two girls on the sand wearing bikinis, nice girls he thinks, with decent figures, full but not too full: he has been watching them all morning. He prefers the brunette, he cannot say why, only that he has always preferred brunettes – the dark, perhaps, that gives shape and meaning to the light. He will wait, he always does, until an opportunity presents itself, he does not like to impose, he is, despite his inflated brain and occasional aggression, strangely shy, he will wait and he will, as always at first, act courteously – one thing his mother, the person in the

The Island

world he at once most hates and loves, has instilled in him. Old-fashioned courtesy. When did it ever come amiss? Though he may act like Elvis, thrusting out a knee in a strange discoordinated style upon the dance floor, flipping back his hair, chortling with a laugh he had learned from the movies, he is not Elvis. Or perhaps he is: was not Elvis also a southern gentleman?

But until then. Nordic, bony and slender, not old but no longer young, fit, almost ascetic, a drinker but rarely drunk, a man whose only desire was to get on with the world, whose only capability was not to, he was at an angle to the world as he was to himself, he was part of the world until he ceased to be part of it: there in the end he would make his bed and lie upon it. But for now his bed was a patch of sand upon an Aegean island where he would live for the summer and watch girls and meditate – where his past would rise up and fill him and he would attempt to process it with a brain capable only of processing symbols.

God was one such. His father another. Unbidden, standing before him. Tall, taller even than him, his only son (there was a much older daughter, his half-sister, whom he never saw). Hunched, angled, his brown eyes beady with enquiry and apprehension, yet demanding, demanding entry into the home he and his mother had built. Standing there on the doorstep. At first he mistook him for a stranger: then, without a word, he knew. And without a word drew back his fist and punched him as hard as he could in the face and closed the door.

His mother standing behind him, turning to him.

Rex?

Ha ha ha, he said, angling his knees and sweeping back his hair with his hand.

Open the door.

No.

She opened it and looked at the man, bleeding from the nose, mopping at the blood with a handkerchief.

Hello Matilda.

You are not welcome here.

No.

He went to the kitchen while his mother and father stared at each other in the doorway. He attempted to make a cup of tea. He spilt sugar over the Formica surface and boiling water on his foot. He hopped up with a shout, clutching his foot in agony. He was dressed in nothing but a pair of underpants. Fuck a duck, he said.

His mother closed the door.

That was your father.

Fuck a duck.

It was the first and only time they met, his only memory. His father went back to wherever he had come from and never returned. He went to London. The crash that had damaged his head even more than it was already damaged behind him. For a few years he lived in London, teaching French and maths in a private tutorial college, sleeping on people's floors, moving with them when they moved until he fell out with them and moved on again. For six months he lived on a sofa in his colleague Bob Spear's living room. He kept his books, his French books and maths books, on the floor behind the sofa. When Bob Spear had guests he went to the pub and sat drinking beer with friends, strangers he had picked up along the way, students who were fascinated by his brain power, his knowledge of maths and history, until one of them, Charlie Garth, found a flat and he moved in with him. He lived there for eighteen months, living, as he preferred, in the sitting room, keeping his books on the floor or in the fridge, until Charlie Garth abandoned the place. He let out the single bedroom to a sailor called Murphy whom he met one night in the pub. And every summer hitch-hiked to Greece to spend two months living on the beach. He was living, though he did not know it, in the way he was supposed to live, the way God planned it.

He was fond of Pascal, especially his wager: it made him chortle with laughter. Best to believe, just in case. But the whole God thing is just an invention, necessary once but no longer –

God died in 1889. Better to be safe than sorry. Besides, what did Nietzsche know? He too was half crazy.

The girls rise. The blonde and the brunette. His eyes are immediately drawn to the brunette: slightly taller than her friend, a little angular, a little more awkward. Like Black Jenny, his one and only one-night stand. His great-aunt, aunt Lena, who had been, like him, homeless, coming to stay with them in London, days that turned into weeks then months, until she reduced the girls living in the back room to tears and had to go. Aunt Lena telling Charlie Garth: he threw a chair at her, you know. Why? She'd upset him somehow, probably without realising. He can't control himself. He was injured – his great-aunt putting her hand up to her head – up here. There were six of them in the Mini and he was in the back – his head went through the roof. The passenger in the front seat was killed, the driver scarred for life. His head went through the roof: now his genius was complemented by brain damage. He had no memory of the crash: now he had no memory of the chair. But throw a chair he did. Aunt Lena sighed: it was his one chance. She was a nice girl. But he threw a chair at her and that was that. He's had other girlfriends but none that lasted. He's too…chivalrous. It's as though he's out of time or stuck in a time warp. Coming in to the kitchen, an empty space hollowed out of the bowels of the earth, trying to cook a fried egg, scattering it all over the floor. Long hard strands of organic pasta boiled in a pan and eaten directly, without the intervention of a plate, sometimes without even a fork. Mysterious spreads eaten on bread. Organic pasta, legumes and beans. Water and beer.

They stand for a moment like sentinels of light, the blonde more rounded, fleshier, better bosomed, wearing nothing but bikinis. The brunette brushing her long dark hair out of her eyes as she addresses the blonde. What are they deciding? he wonders. Before he can wonder further they advance towards the sea. But they do not swim: they walk liltingly, beguilingly, along the seashore, their feet barely touching the water. One bends down and scoops up water in the direction of the other. They laugh and run.

His mother. There, unbearably there, in the flat in Oxford in which he was raised after his father abandoned them. Worn down with sorrow, too old to attract a new mate. Just the two of them. Rex, skinny, violent and angular as the day is long or the sky black: an ageing woman with no life of her own and nothing left to do except entertain her strange seedling, avoid his fists, try to instil in him some sense of right and wrong. The Catholic Church. The Church had clear ideas about right and wrong: her seedling, she sometimes thought, understood none of them.

If God did not exist we would have to invent him.

Well, we have invented him.

Does that mean he exists?

As much as anything exists.

What about the sun, the sand and the sky?

They come and go. Next minute they will all disappear. But God – the true God – is eternal. And he judges. Watches every one of us with his all-seeing eye and, believe you me, he judges.

Now they are sitting at the edge of the sea on the wet sand, the water lapping against their legs and thighs. He props himself up on his elbows. He is proud of his muscular frame, his streamlined torso, the taut muscles visible beneath the skin. Proud of his strength, though his strength has done nothing but lead him into disaster.

Now they are dipping their fingers in the sand like oystercatchers. And talking.

What is there to talk about? Just gossip. Wants and needs expressed or unexpressed. Nothing really said. Just a string of distortions, however hard we try. There is no truth that can be grasped: as soon as it is uttered it becomes a lie. A dazzling string of lies stretching from one end of the universe to the other. A hand's breadth for God, an eternal journey for the rest of us, broken only by death. We shall break the journey, the travellers do solemnly declare, not realising their journey is already over.

He lives on bread and fruit, pasta and miso when he can find it. He has enough money for the summer. A sleeping bag and a bedroll. When the sun finally disappears he will remain on the sand a little longer, with a bottle of cheap wine or a can of beer, then retire to his spot amidst the dunes, sheltered from the world, unroll his bedroll and climb into his bag. He will watch the night insects flicker in the moonlight, listen to the fish prowling and rising beneath the waves, watch the night birds swoop in pursuit of creatures he can no longer see. He might read by torchlight, the metaphysics of Teilhard de Chardin, the morals of Spinoza, before letting the air and the night, the sky and the moon, take him. He will sleep undisturbed, entirely relaxed, until dawn: even then, as the light breaks over the sea, he will sleep. He will sleep within dreams, for to sleep is to dream: he will see his mother, his father, Bob Spear, Charlie Garth. Charlie Garth's grinning face as he makes off with another girl, becomes embroiled, finally shakes himself free. He does not become embroiled. Sometimes he will sleep with a girl in the dunes, more often not. The relationships never last. Time passes, that is all. Here, for the only time, he can escape time. Sleep, eat, lie dreaming upon the sand. Like a long-legged fly upon the stream, dancing an angular dance, not knowing why. Time will pass, he will go back: but he has gone back so many times going back holds no fear. He will, as always, be the last to leave. He will pack up his house and leave like a bird when the weather turns. He lives not for himself, as it may appear, but as a sacrifice for the world. He does not disdain the world: the world chains him as surely as it chained Prometheus.

The girls rise and walk side by side along the seashore, their feet in the water. Will they swim? Should he introduce himself? He imagines it: Hi, I'm Rex, shuffling back his hair, grinning his idiot grin. I'm Rex. Everything is forgotten. The girls turn and smile at him; the brunette's eyes linger upon his face. I'm Rex, he says, over and over again, unable to think of anything else to say. I'm

Dreams and Deceptions

Rex. Yes, we know. You're Rex. An introduction. What are your names? What does it matter? It couldn't matter less, just some name their parents plucked out of the air in the depths of the night without rhyme or reason, some name that attaches itself to them for the duration of their lives: and yet the name is everything. I'm Rex. Why Rex? Who came up with that, his mother or his father? His mother, he presumes. Rex. King? That he would be a king. The purity of the name: the purity of the king. I am, quite simply, a king. Lord of all I survey. There is nothing else to know. Then what? Invite them for a drink? Invite one of them for a drink? Why would they, or she, want to have a drink with him, a man in his early forties living rough on a beach in Greece? I'm Rex, he might say, piteously. Have mercy upon me. Have mercy upon you? It is the highest quality. And if we say no, what then?

He went back to his mother's flat in Oxford. He had run out of places to stay in London, been sacked from his job at the tutorial college, where he had been a popular teacher, quite unlike the other teachers, where he would laugh and brush back his hair, uncertain, engage with the students in a way the other teachers couldn't; where he would stand before the blackboard, cigarette smouldering, legs angled like Elvis, a piece of white chalk in his hand and write with sudden decisiveness upon the board: Le guerre. War: a condition of existence. One of the girls spoke up: War is feminine. Le guerre? La guerre? He wrote both versions on the board, stood back and pondered. The class was divided – the boys for one, the girls for the other. But how can war, with its intrinsic masculinity, its rampant maleness, possibly be feminine? La guerre, said the girl firmly. War is feminine. He stood uncertain, poised between the two possibilities, then scrubbed 'le guerre' from the board. La guerre. It was decided: war was feminine. Now, homeless and jobless, he was once again living with his mother, the mother who did not want him there, who could not understand his unfathomable mind, his litany of complaints about the world: London is impossible, the air is deadly, people have lost the art of communication. Nowhere to live, impossible to find a job. But why, if you have the best brain of your generation, damaged or undamaged? Mother, they do not understand me. What is there to understand? Then Charlie Garth, standing at the door to his mother's flat. He opened the door. Come in, he said. They sat in the kitchen. His mother made tea. He pushed the tea away in disgust. It's too hot, he said. He sat, petulant as a child, the tea halfway across the table, while Charlie Garth sat opposite him. Why can't you make it so I can drink it? he said.

The girls return. They flop down and sit by their baskets. They put on sunglasses, take fruit from a basket and prepare to eat. They are, it seems, unaware of him: so many voices, so many children, so many coloured balls, so many bodies soaking up the sun at the southernmost point of Europe: the sun that floats each morning from the east until it stands above them, dazzling them, burning them with its relentless heat. A breeze springs up from somewhere and is as suddenly gone. Children's voices scatter like confetti in the wind. A long-haired boy picks up a guitar and starts to play. He closes his eyes and dreams. His mother coming to him where he lay in bed, still a child, weeping and screaming. Soothing him. His mother visiting him in hospital, his head bandaged, one leg in a cast. You brought it on yourself. How could I have, I wasn't even driving! You brought it on yourself, she says sternly. He brought it on himself. Every inch crossed, slow as a tortoise, to the point where two paths met: and he, typically, chose the wrong one. What did I bring upon myself, mother? You brought it on yourself, she says, her voice fading, her visage too, everything about her fading except her scent.

Voices float through the air on a gentle breeze. The girls' voices; a family spread out on the sand, the man talking in rapid-fire, gibberish it seems to him, the mother interjecting, softly and calmly: point, counterpoint, a familial harmony. He hears Wagner playing somewhere in the sky and sees, when he opens his eyes for a moment, chariots of fire drawn by horses of stone galloping through the clouds in the cloudless sky. La guerre: of course war is feminine: the birth of the phoenix, the cleansing: nothing is lost. Not even the particles that comprise him, they too will turn to fire and be reborn. Everything is reborn: nothing is. Nothing is except that it passes and is reborn. Yet what is this moment if not the eternal moment?

Drink your tea, says Charlie Garth. Stop complaining.
She always makes it too hot.
Why didn't you ask for milk?
I don't take milk.
Take milk. For heaven's sake. Cool it down. Then drink it.
They drive to Cheltenham in Charlie Garth's car, spend one night in a youth hostel: he lies in his bunk, giggling and chortling, explaining, or trying to explain, how the world works. See, everyone takes what they can for their nearest and dearest; except that the greatest strain, the greatest war, is always with your nearest and dearest. You only hurt, only kill, the ones you love. Love is the precursor of war. Love first then war to the death. Everything is predicated upon this truth.
You need to search the heavens, says Charlie Garth.
It's the same up there, he says. Endless cycles of love and war. Love and war and infidelity. Nothing stays still, not even love.
Where does that leave us?
Here and now, he says.

He opens his eyes. The beach is deserted. Not a soul to be seen: just sky and waves and birds, flocks of white birds fluttering over the water, calling with mewlish cries. Then, as his eyes become accustomed to the light, the beach fills up again: young families, travellers, children: the two girls. They are still there, sitting up, their meal finished, gazing out to sea. What are they looking for? What are they seeing? His eyes follow theirs: there is, as far as

The Island

he can tell, nothing there. Just a tramp steamer on the horizon, a fishing boat halfway from the shore. The birds; and, beyond them, more birds, larger birds, fluttering and diving.

He closes his eyes.

That night in the hostel. Two girls. A slim one and a plump one. He standing, one leg angled, brushing back his hair with his hand, giggling nervously. The plump one talking and smiling, the slim one quieter, more watchful: Charlie Garth's type. They went out into the moonlight, the slim girl and Charlie Garth, leaving him with the plump one: explaining the world to her, relishing the words. Did she fancy him? It was the last thing on his mind. She wasn't his type. He befriended her. They would swap addresses: she would provide him with something he lacked.

Now the girls are applying sun oil to their arms and legs. The blonde loosens her bikini top to allow the brunette to rub oil into her back. He watches transfixed: the brunette's hands on her friend's skin, her hands sliding over her bare shoulders, her fingers running up and down her spine: her friend sitting quite still on the sand gazing, it seems to him, at nothing. We are what we are, there is nothing to be afraid of. His gaze lingering on the blonde's naked back and the brunette's arching body as it rises and falls with the effort of rubbing. Now the blonde turns and, for the first time, notices him.

She smiles. He returns her smile, her face crinkling boyishly. Having smiled, she turns away again.

What, he thinks, would a young girl like that want with a man like me?

Every summer he comes to this island. In the early days he made friends easily: now he is lucky if he hooks up with anyone. Before the crash it was different. But the crash happened: for two years he couldn't even sit in a car. For two years it was all he could do to leave the house until he left the house and went to London. To find himself. But what did he find? Only Bob Spear, Charlie Garth and, for one night, Black Jenny.

You should care more.

Dreams and Deceptions

  I care about you – your lack of purpose and direction.
  Don't worry about me.
  You need to get a hold of yourself – get a job, settle down with someone. That nice brunette from the youth hostel.
  O her, says Charlie Garth. That was a one night stand.

Birds are diving all around him. The girls are lying flat on the sand, the blonde face down, her bikini top untied, the brunette face up, wearing shades, her hand shielding her eyes from the sun. The sun beats down remorselessly: beyond the horizon, a heat haze where nothing is visible. Not the tramp steamers, the diving birds, the passenger liners. Within silence, a silence that rings in his ears, that almost deafens him: a silence that supersedes sound, that obliterates sound, until the sounds are no more than pinpricks in a vast black velvet cloth. Pinpricks of sound, the cries of men and birds intermingling, until even they fade into nothing and there is nothing except the deafening silence.

His mother left Oxford and moved to Cheltenham. Two years later she died. He lay on a bed with a missing leg, propped up by bricks, his possessions scattered over the floors of various rooms, the drawers emptied. Newspapers from the fifties, clothes from the sixties, shoes from the seventies. His eyes closed. A record playing, Bach or Mozart. Then opening his eyes to find Charlie Garth standing there.
  You came.
  The door was open.
  But you came.
  I've a friend with me. How are you?
  He rises and stands in his stockinged feet. Giggling nervously, brushing back his hair.
  People in this town don't know how to live. I'm sick of this town. The air here is rotten.
  I've a friend with me. Shall I bring her up?
  Yes. Yes.

The Island

Two of them, Charlie Garth and another. A small brunette with a freckled face and a wide smile.

He brushes back his hair, his feet tapping out a rhythm on the carpet.

Would you like a cup of tea? Cup of tea?

The freckled girl does not speak.

Thank you, says Charlie.

Good good. I don't have any milk.

Do you have tea?

Lapsang souchong. It's the only tea I can drink now. I can't drink strong tea any more.

That'll be fine, says Charlie.

There is nowhere to sit and so they sit on the bed, papers and clothes scattered on the floor around them. He comes back with tea on a tray.

I've found some sugar. Though you don't really need sugar with lapsang.

How are you?

I fell off my bike. I broke my ankle. He shows them his bare ankle. Here, you can still see the scar. I used to cycle for twenty miles a day, to Prinknash and back.

You went there every day?

Yes, yes, to Prinknash and back. I haven't been able to cycle for nearly two months. This town is wearing me down. People here don't know how to live. The air is rotten.

They sip their tea.

Do you still go to Greece every summer?

Yes. Most summers, yes.

Will you be going this summer?

That was the last time he saw him. And the girl. Charlotte or Caroline or some such. She was pretty, that was true. She had some sort of history, had been in prison for fraud, some case connected with a murder. Her mother had murdered her father, something of that sort. He opens his eyes and closes them again.

Dreams and Deceptions

I am Rex. I am Rex. Rex Warner Shillingstone. The last of the Shillingstones. The blonde girl has turned her head and is looking straight at him but as far as he can tell cannot see him. Perhaps he should ask her out. Perhaps he should ask them both out. It's the brunette he fancies. Perhaps he should ask her out. Perhaps he will. There are people around him now. The two girls. A young family. Mother and father and two young children. The children are playing in the sand. They are Greek. As for the two girls, they could be anything – Greek, English, Swedish, Israeli. They don't look Greek. They are tourists like him. Not tourists, travellers. Are you travellers? he might say. Do we look like travellers? they might reply.

The sun pours down like melted honey. People are melting in the heat. The two girls have changed places: now the blonde lies on her back, the brunette on her front. The young family has fallen silent, the children lie listlessly upon the sand. The birds still fly and the fish still swim. He is almost exactly halfway through his life.